---THE ~~~~~~
ROUGE-------

----geoff
small----

Digital edition first published in 2013
Published by The Electronic Book Company
www.theelectronicbookcompany.com

research and study.

Please note: *The Dirty Rouge* was written, produced and edited in the UK where some of the spellings and word usage vary slightly from U.S. English.

CONTENTS:

Introduction

D.C.I Patrick Curzon is the 'Dirty Rouge'.

A thief, a blackmailer, a ruthless politician, this tough, misanthropic Scotsman is one of the vilest cops to have ever graced the page. That said, he's also one of the most dedicated.

While investigating the death of a young 'schemie', Curzon paces the streets of his beloved Glasgow, conversing with junkies, small time coke dealers, a millionairess and even a premier league footballer. The case also brings him back into conflict with his sworn enemy, Fergus Baxter, a highly vaunted though particularly sleazy defence lawyer who acts on behalf of the city's most lucrative violent psychopaths and any celebrities who happen to fall through the cracks into criminality.

As the truth unravels, Curzon finds himself caught between the interests of justice and those of the local establishment, leaving him with a major dilemma.

Language: UK English Spellings

---THE DIRTY ROUGE-------

----geoff small----

Chapter 1

DCI Patrick Curzon stumbled down the steps from Nancy's townhouse. He staggered across the street to a park, where he slumped on a bench and smoked a cigarette while enjoying the June dawn chorus. At just five-foot-nine, this forty-year-old Scotsman had short black curly hair, a pug nose and deep brown eyes which wouldn't have looked out of place on a ventriloquist's doll. Shoulders hunched, a sullen, spiteful sneer, his whole body exuded the malice that bred within, warding off all but the most foolhardy. Having no friends to speak of, he lived in a one bed-roomed apartment on Gardner Street, cluttered with all the bric-a-brac he'd stolen over the years, not only from the homes of criminals, but from the houses of witnesses and even the families of murder victims. This included a half-knitted jumper with the needles still attached, a prosthetic leg and would you believe, a stuffed racing pigeon. This may not sound too outrageous, until, that is, you factor in forty-three suitcases, twelve holdalls and three backpacks full of luggage, all snatched from the various transport terminuses around Glasgow while in the course of his duties – not to mention a drawer load of phones, which he always took as a matter of principle if left unattended. It wasn't that he was a kleptomaniac, he just enjoyed inconveniencing people. That said, he always waited for folk to commit some slight before resorting to robbery, thus absolving himself on the basis he was discharging justice. However, he actively provoked people into treating him badly by behaving in a fashion that he knew would elicit their worst side, for which he then made them pay – forever. Without doubt, this spitefulness emanated from his childhood, when he'd been taunted by the whole school as 'The Dirty Rouge' because of his alcoholic father's impoverishing taste for red Buckfast wine, an affliction which had left Curzon a neglected boy wandering the streets in unwashed rags. Then, he'd dreamed of becoming a policeman so that he could arrest each and every one of his persecutors and lock them away for the rest of their lives.

Abandoned by a clinically depressed mother and ostracised by his peers, Curzon had spent his free time as a child hanging around libraries, reading the works of Raymond Chandler and Mickey Spillane, before wandering the city centre's hilly grid plan at night, peeking his little head in at bar-room doors and fantasising that he was Phillip Marlow or Mike Hammer. To this day their noir aesthetic had stayed with him and was exemplified during the winter months by a beige Burberry trench coat, which he donned with undisguised pride. Even the location of his apartment – in a tenement on one of Glasgow's steepest streets – had been chosen simply because of its resemblance to San Francisco, where some of his favourite fictional detectives had lived and worked.

You'd have thought with such chivalrous characters as role models, Curzon would have ended up of a more philanthropic disposition, but his non-fiction reading saw that their influence was heavily diluted, incorporating as it did anything on Niccolò Machiavelli, Joseph Stalin or, his personal favourite, J. Edgar Hoover: the FBI's director who had dirt on the whole population of America. The end result of such a dubious education was a streetwise politician with the drop on everyone, including his superiors. Everybody, from his chief superintendent down to the local junkie, lived in terror of the evidence he had horded away at lawyers' offices up and down the land, ready to be disseminated the moment anything untoward befell him. As a consequence he was loathed by criminals and colleagues alike, but he was an incredible detective who lived and breathed the streets of Glasgow each second of the day.

***

Sat at his bench in his dark grey Armani suit and black polo T-shirt, Curzon had just finished a cigarette when his phone rang. It was Detective Constable George McKay requesting his presence down at Largs, thirty miles away along the Firth of Clyde, where the body of a young man had washed up on the beach. Curzon, who hadn't slept in nearly twenty-four hours, was still way too drunk to drive, so he asked McKay to send him someone from uniform in a squad car, which arrived five minutes later, blue light flashing. What with the empty roads at that time of morning and the ability to speed at one hundred and thirty miles an hour with impunity, it took just fifteen minutes to reach the seafront, from where Curzon could see a huddle of people down near the shoreline, silhouetted against a white sky that made the whole world feel like the inside of a Tupperware box. Leaving his driver in the car, he crunched across the pebbles in his brown suede shoes towards the group, which stood about ten feet from a corpse and an eight-foot pine log, both having become enmeshed somehow in an orange fishing net.

'I assume that floated down from Glasgow with the rest of the shite,' he shouted as he approached, causing Detective Sergeant Denise Deegan to flash him a disapproving stare, while a woman police officer escorted the horrified old lady who'd found the body away, a sorry-looking poodle in her arms.

Curzon continued past the group and crouched down beside the fish-netted cadaver. Tasselled with seaweed, the body was clad in denim jeans, a navy-blue T-shirt and a backpack containing concrete bricks, its crew cut hair black, its alabaster face, though now swollen and covered in goose bumps after having been immersed in saltwater for so long, probably good-looking once. The most distinguishing feature, though, on the young man's right forearm, a St. Clyde F.C

Tattoo with 'BOBBY' underneath.

'Forensics will be here shortly sir. But as you can already see by what's in the backpack, someone definitely didn't want us to find him,' proffered Denise, who was now standing directly behind Curzon, looking pretty alluring in a dove grey pinstriped trouser suit, which accentuated her tall, svelte, twenty-seven-year-old body and set off her shoulder-length blonde bobbed hair and piercing blue eyes.

Curzon stood up from his haunches and turned to Denise scratching his head, his puffy eyes squinting in the morning light, the salty, sea air penetrating his stale skin and making his booze-soaked bones feel brittle.

'So how the hell did we find him anyway, after someone went to so much trouble?'

'We spoke to an old beach comber before you arrived, a guy in his seventies who just happens to have once been Professor of Oceanography at Aberdeen University. He says that forty percent of the stuff that washes up on this shore is from North America, and that the log in the fishing net has come all the way from Canada. He even offered to bet me a hundred pound that somebody's most probably dumped the corpse off a boat in the dead of night, unaware that it's gone straight into the path of this log, where it's got caught up in the attached net and then been brought straight back to shore…Basically, if they'd chucked it ten seconds earlier, or ten seconds later even, it'd be at the bottom of the sea now.'

Denise and her boss suddenly started laughing at the darkly comedic, bizarre absurdity of the whole thing.

'Wait till whoever's done this see's the news tonight,' Curzon gloated, 'they'll choke on their Special Brew, so they will,'

'It's pure chaos theory when you think about it sir. Some moustachioed lumberjack in Newfoundland ties his load a little too loosely, then, a month later, at precisely the wrong moment, one of his logs bobs up two thousand miles away and ruins a perfect murder in Scotland. It'll probably be the cause of a war too, coz this is definitely Glasgow gangland…professional stuff sir. But for that piece of timber 'Bobby with a St. Clyde tattoo' would have been just another missing person.'

'I hope to Christ you're right Denise, coz I don't want to spend a minute longer than I have to in this godforsaken place.'

Hands buried deep in his suit jacket pockets, shoulders hunched even more than usual against the sea breeze, he turned, wincing, to face the wet-looking green hills which loomed behind the short promenade of red sandstone and whitewashed buildings, framed by a gothic church spire at either end. To a city boy like Curzon, this was hell.

Forensics had turned up by now, so the three detectives left them to it and repaired to a cafe on the front, which had kindly opened two hours early to cater for the ever- increasing entourage of policemen. Deegan and McKay had coffee and toast, while Curzon, who sat opposite, ate a full cooked breakfast, slurping his tea and masticating his food with such slow deliberation it were as if he were interrogating each morsel. Not only that, but he smacked his lips together the whole time, causing Deegan teeth-grinding irritation, which, she suspected, was the whole purpose of his exaggeratedly bad table manners.

Having cleaned up the plate with his last morsel of fried bread, Curzon licked the grease from his fingers then sucked on his teeth.

'Right, I've to be in court this morning for a verdict. No doubt by the time I've come out we'll know who exactly 'Bobby' is.' Deegan and McKay nodded. 'Then we'll start with his mammy and daddy and work our way out from there, picking up as much shite as we can on everyone, innocent or guilty. And if it looks like it's going to be too easy to solve, then we'll deliberately begin somewhere right off the mark. Remember, murders are our opportunity to legitimately stir nests we couldn't otherwise disturb and to gather knowledge about as many citizens as possible.'

At this point Curzon had to answer his phone.

'DCI Curzon.' He listened for about three seconds and then jumped up from his chair. 'Come on you two!'

Deegan and McKay sprang up and hurried out of the cafe behind their boss, who jogged down the promenade until he'd reached his chauffeur-driven squad car.

'What is it sir?!' Deegan asked, gasping for breath.

'Avoiding paying for that breakfast, hen, that's what it is! Now, I'm away back to mine for a shower. I'll catch you later on.'

And with that he climbed back into the squad car, which tore off at high speed again, blue light flashing.

Chapter 2

Curzon had enjoyed a good weekend. On Sunday, he'd finally succeeded in pinning an attempted murder charge on a villain he'd been pursuing for over ten years – hence the party round at Nancy's that night – and on the Friday morning before, he'd managed to derail an exquisite defence case at the High Court, turning the prosecution's lot from lost-cause to hanging in the balance. However, this had required some serious skulduggery. Just as the defence team's unscheduled, last minute alibi had arrived in the building, Curzon had intercepted the woman and deliberately shepherded her to the wrong waiting room. While doing so, he'd sent a sneaky text message from one of his many stolen phones. This served as a signal for the recipient to make a hoax emergency call to the defence advocate's clerk, who, in turn, had handed the court usher an urgent note, which was passed to her boss just as he was about to request the judge's permission for a final, wild card witness. On reading the letter, the advocate had literally run from the courtroom, without explanation, causing an adjournment. How was he to know that his six-year-old daughter hadn't really been run over at all, or that the phone call hadn't come from a hospital social worker, but that it was in fact made by a junkie from Calton? Of course, by the time he'd found out, it was too late. With every designated piece of testimony having been heard, the judge had already told the prosecution to prepare their closing statement. As a consequence, nobody got to hear that the defendant wasn't even in Glasgow on the date of the alleged baseball bat attack, or that he'd actually been in Dundee all day, making love to his sister-in-law. Yes, the accused was a notorious thug who'd been terrorizing folk for years, but on this particular count he was completely and utterly innocent. Tiny details such as these made no odds to Curzon though. According to him, it was far sweeter to convict a professional criminal for something he hadn't done, rather than for everything he had. Not only that, but it was also a damn sight easier.

It sounds incredible that every unpredictable aspect of Curzon's plan should just fall into place like this. Truth is, the hoax call had been a total gamble. No one could have known how the advocate, a highly professional man, would have reacted to the emotional bait.

As for the judge, well, Curzon had already been told by Nancy that he'd be retiring after this case, and that he was impatient to get it over before the weekend. Why? Because Judge Lord Douglas Roper was due to start a new career on the lucrative after-dinner speaking circuit the following week, adding two-thousand pound per appearance to his sixty-five-thousand-pound pension. Least to say, he'd been pretty angry when the jury had failed to reach a verdict, necessitating their stay at the Crown Plaza hotel until the Monday morning, when everyone would have to return and try again, while his plane left for Toronto without him.

It wasn't necessarily the defendant that Curzon was willing to risk his career on seeing defeated, so much as the person representing him, and in this case it wasn't the advocate himself but the lawyer he worked for. His name was Fergus Baxter, a highly vaunted though particularly sleazy defence lawyer who acted on behalf of the city's most lucrative violent psychopaths and any celebrities who happened to fall through the cracks into criminality. This smirking, gnome-like, ginger-haired, goatee-bearded, brown-and-green-tartan-suited mobster's mouthpiece had excited Curzon's ire after having successfully defended a drunken banker by the name of Maker, who'd mown down two schoolboys in his Porsche, which was later found torched on a council housing scheme. If he'd been beaten fair and square, Curzon would have accepted that. But the verdict had been highly dubious. In the face of endless circumstantial evidence, four eyewitnesses and three items of material proof – which included a cigarette butt with Maker's DNA on it, thrown from the car window, twenty yards from the crime – the judge had still directed the jury to pass a verdict of Not Proven. To add insult to injury, two teenage delinquents whose fingerprints were found on a fuel canister, near to where the burnt-out sports car had been found, were tried and found guilty of manslaughter. Curzon couldn't help but suspect a closing of ranks among high society and his feud with Baxter had become an obsession. That's why he was now willing to delegate urgent preliminary work on the Largs murder inquiry, because he just had to be in court to see the look on his adversary's face if he lost. And lose he did, though this was small fry compared to the Maker case, just a gangster's muscle being found guilty of a serious assault. But Curzon had put his marker down, shown the tartan serpent that he was willing to fight dirty as well, ensuring that both of them now had the bit between their teeth, guaranteeing their next encounter as gargantuan.

Meanwhile, it hadn't been too difficult for DS Deegan and DC McKay to ascertain the identity of a Bobby with a St. Clyde tattoo, what with him being on probation for shoplifting.

Bobby McQueen had lived with his parents in the south-east of the city on Castlemilk, one of four infamous post-war, peripheral housing schemes which occupied each corner of Glasgow. Here, at a first-floor apartment in a grey, pebble-dashed tenement, the two detectives endured the ordeal of informing a mother that she'd lost her only son.

Apart from learning that the deceased had actually been an apprentice at his beloved St. Clyde F.C before getting sacked for stealing from the senior players' dressing room, that his bedroom wall was covered in flyers from the Ménage à Trance nightclub, and observing that the construction site across the road from his house had an abundance of concrete bricks identical to those found in the backpack on his corpse, their inquiries hit a buffer. Yes, they did have the name of his best friend, Craig Hunter, but he was of no fixed abode and, like the deceased, hadn't been seen since Saturday night.

As can well be imagined of such a tight-knit community, trying to get names from people, let alone information, had been virtually impossible. Of course, when they returned to the station that lunchtime and complained about the lack of cooperation from local tenants, Curzon blew his top.

'What?' He put on a whining baby's voice to mock them: 'They – won't – speak – to – us!' Then he sighed furiously. 'Jesus Christ man! Your job is to MAKE them speak to us! You're not selling double glazing…this is a fucking murder inquiry!' He blew his cheeks out. 'Has Craig Hunter got a record?' Deegan shook her head. 'Did you check his extended family out on the computer?'

'Of course,' she snapped indignantly.

'Ah, well, I wonder sometimes. And?'

'Nothing.'

'So that's that then is it? Case closed?' His nose was screwed up now in a snarl, facial muscles taught, teeth in a rictus of rage as he stared demandingly into Deegan's eyes. 'Have you not checked out his buddies list on Facebook?

'Yesss,' she hissed.

'What about girlfriends? Do we know if he has any?'

'I'll get to it.'

Deegan, who was now imagining her inspector's head on a pole, turned and stormed out of the room.

'So how's the other stuff coming along?' Curzon asked McKay.

McKay, who was something of a narcissist, even though he had the face of a gurning Buzzard, ran his left hand through his combed-back brown hair and sighed.

'The initial results from the autopsy say it was a serrated bread knife that inflicted the fatal injury with an upwards thrust. The deceased's also got a broken nose and a lot of bruising, though it's impossible to know whether or not these were caused post-mortem by buffeting from waves or the violence of being swept ashore. As for forensics, they reckon there's no chance of salvaging any evidence, not after a body's been lying in salt water for that length of time. But Scenes of Crime have confirmed the old beach comber's theory: that the corpse got entangled in the fishing net which had become attached to the log, before the log carried both back onto the shore.' Curzon furrowed his brow while trying to keep up with this exposition. 'And of course, we're examining CCTV footage on any routes Bobby McQueen might have taken about town...so that'll probably take us about a year.'

Displeased with this attempt at levity, Curzon stared menacingly at McKay, before leaving the office without a word and walking across town to keep an appointment. Apart from emergencies or logistical necessities, Curzon went everywhere by foot or on public transport because, he argued, it was the only way to have any feel for the streets he was supposed to police. Not only that, but it was amazing what intelligence could be garnered simply by eavesdropping conversations on a bus. His destination on this particular occasion was the Necropolis: Glasgow's great city of the dead, on a hill east of the cathedral.

Chapter 3

Curzon entered the Necropolis through a gap in the railings, before scrambling up a grass slope, past ten-foot-high granite obelisks and sandstone burial chambers that resembled scaled down versions of Greek temples, all overlooked by John Knox on top of his column at the summit. Halfway up, he crept round to the east side of a tall monument where a skinny brunette wearing a white vest and blue, striped Adidas jogging bottoms was sat on the plinth, hugging herself with one arm, pulling and pushing on a cigarette with the other.

'Boo!'

The girl jolted back in terror, dropping her cigarette and banging the back of her head against the hard stone, the impact only softened by the spongy lichens which had grown there. She held a hand against her heaving, flat chest.

'What the fuck did you go and do that for?'

She had the dry croak of a heroin-user and a wizened face that had once been attractive but now looked at least a decade older than its twenty-eight years.

'Well done with the phone call Jackie – went down a treat,' Curzon said, as he sat on the ledge next to her.

She sniffled. 'That mean we're quits then?'

The detective carried on looking straight ahead.

'Jackie? Do you know why a dastardly deed is called a dastardly deed?'

'Eh?' She screwed her face up in bewilderment.

'It's because it's dastardly. And do you know what a dastard is?' She shrugged her shoulders. 'It's a dishonourable or despicable person…and that's what you are, Jackie.' Jackie held her palm to her forehead and sighed dejectedly. 'I'm your conscience and you'll never get rid of me.'

'No you're not, believe me. Do you not think I don't suffer enough for what I did?'

'How do I know what to believe of someone who informs on her own husband in return for a tenner bag of heroin...He served two years for your hour of pleasure.'

'That wasn't evil on my part, you exploited my circumstances...I was rattling.'

'Aye, well, the only way to escape me is to confess to him, and that's not a very good idea, not with his proven prowess with a craft knife. You need to get used to the fact that you're my slave now forever, at least until the day someone inevitably finds you slumped dead in a close with a hypodermic needle sticking out of your groin...And besides, it's not all bad news. You know that whenever you're in trouble with the law you just ask to see me. I always keep you out of court don't I? And make sure you speak to me and only me if anyone asks about Friday's little piece of telephony. Understand?'

Jackie, who was now hugging herself with both arms while rocking back and forth, nodded, sniffling.

'Talking of which,' Curzon clicked his fingers three times demandingly, prompting Jackie to remove a phone from her hip pocket and hand it to him. In return, he produced two magazine paper wraps from the inside pocket of his suit jacket and held them out in an open, flat palm to the desperate young woman. She went to take them but he closed his hand into a fist at the last moment and snatched it away, obnoxiously. 'Ah, ah, ah. I've got another wee job for you. How well do you know Castlemilk?'

'I've been there a few times to score...I've been everywhere to score at one time or another,' she joked, letting out a rasping, smoker's cough of a laugh.

'Right then, today I want you to go on over there and hang about, the pubs, the shops, anywhere where there's anyone. If someone asks, just say you're looking to score some heroin.'

'And the point is?'

'The point is, you just come back and tell me everything you overhear. I don't care if it's snippets of conversations about the local pigeon fancier's sciatica, I want to know everything. I'll meet you back here tomorrow morning at seven, so don't go overdoing it on that shite…you don't want to make me have to come looking for you, drawing attention to the fact that you associate with police officers now do you?'

'Nah.'

Curzon handed her the two wraps along with fifty quid in ten-pound notes.

'Bloody hell, expenses eh?' Jackie gasped. 'This must be important to you.'

'Never you mind. Just don't go wasting any of it until the day's up. It's your cover remember? You're up there to score, so you'll need money to maintain your ruse. There's no need to go blowing it on gear cos I'll have some more for you tomorrow morning anyway.'

And with that the detective chief inspector got up and left.

Chapter 4

On Curzon's return to the station, McKay was waiting with photographs of the bricks used to weigh Bobby McQueen's body down, and an inventory of calls made to the young man's phone in the days leading up to his death. Unsurprisingly, the last received call had come from the elusive best friend, Craig Hunter. But the last call out was intriguing to say the least, having been made to the landline of a certain Ms Matilda Fuchs of Westbourne Gardens in Hyndland, at 9.20pm the Saturday night just gone.

Finally they had something to work on and so, as Deegan and McKay returned to the pebble-dashed council houses of Castlemilk, in another bid to find the whereabouts of Mr Hunter, Curzon made a teatime visit to the home of Ms Fuchs, who lived in a four-floored, blonde sandstone townhouse, complete with basement area railings and broad steps which took you from the roadside up to its shiny black, Georgian front door. From there you could hear that somebody was vacuuming inside and, as a consequence, Curzon had to press the big bell four times before anybody heard. When Ms Fuchs finally answered, he was doubled over her wrought iron balustrade, trying to get a better view of some cigarette butts which had been discarded in the area directly under the steps, their unusual, bright gold-coloured filters having piqued his obsessive curiosity.

'Hello, can I help you?'

Aged about forty, Ms Fuchs had one of those authoritative German accents which Curzon found both aggressive and sexy at the same time. She must have been six foot tall, her long blonde hair tied back in a ponytail, giving full reign to a strong Teutonic face, featuring a prominent nose that he quite liked. Wearing a white vest and black leather trousers, she wiped her brow with her right hand – which contained a duster – drawing attention not only to her powerful, muscular arms but to her copious bosom as well. When Curzon flashed his ID, she squinted to examine it with her baby blue eyes, before deploying them on him.

'Inspector eh?' she said flirtatiously then laughed in a loud, Dracula-esque manner. 'Please, come in…come in!' She turned and led the way into an extravagantly spacious, lily-white interior. 'You must excuse the mess, only we had a party and barbeque on Saturday night and I've only just got round to cleaning up. Too hungover yesterday.'

In the hallway which led to the kitchen, two guilty-looking teenagers wearing jogging bottoms and sports shoes were mopping the chessboard tiled floor.

'OK boys, I think you've done enough for today.' Frau Fuchs took two twenty-pound notes from a leather purse on the phone table and handed one to each of them. 'Don't go spending it on anything naughty now.'

As they left, the detective noticed that one of them sneakily pinched the German's backside, prompting her to playfully swat the back of his head with her duster.

Once the front door had boomed shut behind the boys, Curzon followed Frau Fuchs into a huge sitting room with a high ceiling, where four brown, leather three-seat couches were arranged in a quadrangle around a predominantly red Moroccan rug on a parquet floor, so shiny you could see your reflection in it. She sat down sideways on one of the couches, opposite Curzon, with one leg over the other, so that he was almost mesmerised by the firm shiny black leather peach she was presenting to him.

'So tell me *inspector*, what seems to be the problem?'

And with that playful mockery she started laughing again, before closing her full lips once more so that her suppressed giggle sounded like a creaky door squeaking open. The more Curzon resisted reciprocating her good humour and stared impassively, the more amusing she seemed to find the whole situation.

'Ms Fuchs, have you watched the local news at all today?'

'I don't watch news…too depressing.' She turned her head to the side and dismissively waved the idea away with her right hand.

'Only, an old lady found the body of a nineteen-year-old man down on Largs beach this morning. His name was Bobby McQueen.'

Immediately, Frau Fuchs seemed to shrink, her face lost its playfulness and aged by ten years right there and then. She sat up poker straight, tilted her head to one side and began to shake it.

'Really?' This sounded more like a plea than a question.

'Unfortunately, yes. And his last recorded phone call was to this house at 9.20pm on Saturday night.'

Curzon produced a photo of Bobby McQueen from the inside pocket of his suit jacket and handed it to her. As she took it her long fingers trembled slightly. After studying the picture she closed her eyes, as if trying to hide from the world, then handed it back.

'You know him then Ms Fuchs?'

'No. It's just such a shame, that's all.'

Curzon nodded slowly, disbelieving her.

'You say you had a party here on Saturday? Might he possibly have been one of the guests?'

He held the photograph up in front of her face.

'Possibly. We have many people coming and going…friends of friends, that sort of thing.'

'Do you remember taking a phone-call from anybody unusual?'

'There were lots of calls, not all of them taken by me.'

'Who else might have taken calls then?'

'Whoever was nearest the phone at the time I suppose…it was a party…there were a lot of people helping out,' she replied, irritably.

'OK, so how many people would you say were here on Saturday night, roughly?'

At this point, Frau Fuchs seemed to have fallen into a trance and not heard the question, before she suddenly came to again.

'Erm…fifty…maybe a hundred overall, what with people coming and going, just popping their heads in to say hello, you know.'

While she was talking, Curzon had been eying a framed photograph on a little oak table in the corner, featuring a much younger blonde girl, probably in her late teens.

'Could your husband or anyone else in the family possibly have taken that phone call?'

'I'm divorced,' she said, almost spitting the words out.

Curzon always struggled to suppress a smug smirk when people told him they were divorced, because every failed marriage confirmed his cynical view that human beings could not be trusted and would always let you down.

'Who's the attractive young lady in the photograph over there, your daughter?'

Frau Fuchs looked suddenly extremely frightened and snapped defensively:

'Yes…why?'

'Oh, nothing, I just thought that she might have taken the call, that's all.'

'She's not here at the moment…She's over in Germany with her father.'

'Ah, so she wasn't here on Saturday night then?'

Frau Fuchs hesitated before answering: 'No.'

While asking the woman questions, Curzon had been fiddling with two stolen, reformatted phones in his pocket, so that one rang the other.

'Excuse me.'

He jumped to his feet pretending to answer and, talking loudly to no one, marched out of the sitting room, down the long hallway, its walls decorated to shoulder height with Spanish tiles, then across the chessboard floor of the kitchen – which was so large you could have built a small house in there – until he was in the back garden. Here, empty champagne and wine bottles stood in lines on every available ledge, most strikingly on the walls of the purpose-built barbeque area, which had been constructed from the same concrete bricks as those found in the backpack attached to Bobby McQueen's body, with several spare ones piled up in a wheelbarrow at the far end of the lawn. On the grill, among pale grey cinders, were burnt chops and blackened, expensive-looking gourmet sausages, and, on the floor all about, ketchup and mustard-stained white napkins. One napkin, though, on the patio in front of the barbeque area, aroused particular interest in Curzon. It was smeared in something that was, to him, by now, completely unmistakable. Crouching down, he removed a plastic evidence bag from his inside pocket, picked up a wooden kebab skewer from the floor and impaled the blood-stained tissue, before shaking it into the container. Back when he'd been a rookie, his heart would have been thumping at twenty beats a nanosecond now, adrenaline warming his every limb and sinew like eighteen-year-old single malt whisky hitting your oesophagus. But he'd learnt over the years to remain completely calm and objective and never to let any one clue take precedence in a case, because there was often a simple, innocent explanation for everyday things that had a habit of taking on a sinister appearance when viewed through the prism of a murder inquiry. More importantly, there were very few forensic scientists in the world and so they had to be deployed with surgical precision, while always minding not to bring the city to a standstill for white plastic tents, erected every time some neurotic detective got a hunch about something.

When Curzon returned to the sitting-room, Frau Fuchs was still sat staring into space.

'OK Ms Fuchs, I'm sorry to have disrupted your cleaning. If I could just inconvenience you for one more thing, though?'

'Go on?'

'Overnight, could you maybe sit with a pen and paper and write down the names of as many guests as you can remember who attended on Saturday?' Frau Fuchs nodded in a resigned, tired fashion. 'I'd be very grateful...I mean, the phone call may well turn out to be nothing in the end, but it's a murder inquiry. I'm sure you understand.'

'Yes, yes of course.'

'Thank you. I'll show myself out then.'

And so, Curzon left a demoralised, defensive woman in an evident state of shock who had, just minutes previously, been warm, forthcoming, coquettish and carefree. It was obvious that she had something to hide. That she knew Bobby McQueen, Curzon was in no doubt. But it was also obvious that she'd neither murdered nor conspired to murder anybody, so genuinely shocked was she at hearing of the young man's death.

Chapter 5

It was about seven in the evening when Curzon got back to the station, from where he sent his newfound evidence off to the lab. Then he told Deegan and McKay to get off home, neither having managed to ascertain any new information during their trawls around Castlemilk.

What with being at the casino and Nancy's until past four the previous night, then being called to the body on the beach at Largs, the detective chief inspector hadn't slept in over thirty-six hours. Before going home, though, he took a metallic grey Ford Mondeo from the police compound and headed across town for some groceries. Having already given his final fifty pounds to Jackie, he was too broke to be able to visit a supermarket, so travelled three miles out of his way, driving through the Clyde tunnel and into a conspicuously Asian neighbourhood on the Southside. Here, he went into Sharma's convenience shop, nestled in the middle of an iron shuttered parade, beneath a beautiful, sandstone tenement, which radiated every shade and hue of blonde in the evening sunshine.

Having been the community's purveyor of cigarettes, booze and newspapers for over thirty years, Mr Sharma was a respected feature in the neighbourhood, a comforting piece of continuity in a gratuitously fast changing world. Everybody addressed him as Mr Sharma and he in turn knew all his regular customers names and saluted them with the same quaint courtesy. Once he knew you, you were welcome to credit and if you were short of cash he always let you off the difference and just dismissed the whole situation with a philosophical, backward wave of the hand, as if swatting a gnat.

As Curzon entered Sharma's twilit emporium, the man himself, tall and well-fed with big, round, naïve looking eyes, stood joking with an old lady as he filled her shopping bags for her on the counter, before coming round to walk her out of the shop. On spotting the detective, though, his mirth disappeared and, after watching the old lady safely to her tenement from the door, he walked back to his post forlornly, head down, while his visitor filled a basket with a four-pack of McEwen's Export Lager, two meat feast pizzas, a bag of oven fries and a block of Neapolitan ice cream. As

Curzon approached the counter, Sharma turned as if by telepathy and took forty Berkeley cigarettes and a bottle of Glenfiddich from the shelves behind him, which he then bagged up along with the food, without going near the cash register and without uttering a single word to his *customer* or even making eye contact. Basically, it was a petty extortion racket, enforced by Curzon following an incident two years previously when he'd been caught stealing a ninety-nine pence toothbrush by the shop owner. Of course, back then, Sharma didn't have any idea that he was dealing with a detective chief inspector, and when he'd found out, after Curzon had flashed his ID – in the same aggressive manner that a criminal might pull a gun – he'd been even more adamant that the police be called and had locked our hero in the store. At this point Curzon had invoked moral relativism, snatching at a single pack of Kleenex tissues on a nearby shelf, on which were printed the words: ONLY TO BE SOLD IN MULTI-PACK. Next, he'd taken a shot in the dark, telling Sharma that he knew all about the smuggled cigarettes and alcohol he was selling and not paying tax on, prompting the grocer to unlock and open the door, standing poker straight in a bid to retain some dignity as the detective strode out of the dimly-lit shop to freedom, brandishing and waving the stolen toothbrush triumphantly. If Sharma had thought that would be the end of the matter, he was wrong. According to Curzon's thinking, the Indian had had no intention of showing him any mercy when on top, and so now, he was obliged to return the same lack of compassion. As extortion rackets go it was small-time: a four-pack of ale, a bottle of malt whisky, forty cigarettes and a meal's worth of convenience food once a week. That said, it probably amounted to about fifteen hundred pounds annually, not to mention the humiliation the shopkeeper had to endure. But he certainly wasn't the only one. Curzon must have had a score of corner shops, restaurants and fast food takeaways in his palm, meaning that he never had to pay for any of his food or drink. However, it also meant that he hadn't eaten anything remotely healthy in years.

Back at his apartment, Curzon sat in the tiny cluttered front room wearing only his boxer shorts, tray on lap, deliberately chewing each morsel of pizza, sucking on each greasy oven fry and slurping on his can of McEwen's, before taking a very large helping of malt to bed with him, where he lay on top of the covers deliberating over the case so far, enjoying a much-savoured sip of the golden nectar every two minutes or so. It must be pointed out here that, unlike his father, the detective was by no means an alcoholic. Considering the booze-related misery of his upbringing, though, you're probably surprised he had any taste for the stuff at all. Indeed, the issue of drink had provided a real dilemma for Curzon as a teenager. No, he most definitely did not want to end up like his old man, but he also knew that he could never whole-heartedly emulate his fictional heroes if he wasn't to quaff a few shots of the hard stuff from time to time.

Once he'd finally drained the last drop from the glass tumbler, of which he had dozens, all stolen from the city's pubs, Curzon was almost relaxed enough to sleep. I say almost because never, since the age of thirteen, had he been able to settle down to rest without masturbating first. He didn't use porn, just his imagination, based on real women he'd seen around town, like Frau Fuchs and Jackie the Junkie. On this occasion, after several minutes of deliberation, he decided to cast the latter as leading lady in that night's fantasy. Ultimately, Frau Fuchs had proved too vulnerable a human being, but Jackie was tough as old boots, which was precisely how he liked his women. And so, boxer shorts round his ankles, fist clenched tight round his erect penis, he pumped his hand, getting faster and more intense all the time, breathing through his nostrils like an angry Bull as, in his mind, he took Jackie the Junkie from behind while she kneeled naked on all fours on top of a knee-high, lichened grave slab in the Necropolis, her bony, milky white arse cold against his own sharp hip bones. All the time, his eyes focused on the green, tattooed love heart on the back of her right shoulder, containing the name of the husband she'd had sent down, a diagonal cupid's arrow piercing through it.

'Arghhhhhhh…you dirty bastard! You dirty, fucking pig bastard!' she screamed, then sighed huskily, ecstatically, half-soaked in opiates, as he went round to the other end of the slab and pulled her face onto his tumescence, by her shoulder length, greasy brown hair. She went down on it aggressively, hungrily gulping his body salts with every backward motion of her head, her sunken cheeks made even more hollow by the action, her plaque-mottled teeth occasionally abrasive against his soft foreskin, making him all the more aroused in the process, before he withdrew and, wanking, held the area beneath his glans tight, so that his ejaculate squirted like Cobra venom onto her sweating face, one globule hanging like a dew drop from the end of her button nose. Simultaneously, Curzon ejaculated in the real world too, heart thudding like a dance track bass line, lungs panting like an Everest summiteer's, his sinuses and any stress behind the eyes clearing momentarily as he just lay there, taking long, deep breaths.

Chapter 6

Next thing Curzon knew he was being woken by a crack of thunder at six-thirty in the morning, ankles still manacled by his boxer shorts. Running his tongue around his whisky-stale mouth, he listened to the rain clattering on the street outside until he suddenly remembered that he had to meet Jackie. He leapt up, showered and put on his grey suit and beige trench coat, before driving over to the Necropolis. After squeezing through the gap in the railings, he scrambled up the greasy, wet bank, slipping here and there, the rain drops running down his nose thick as tears. Rounding the ten-foot-high tomb he prepared himself for a no-show but was shocked to find a purple, one-man tent pitched on the grass, the rain patting loudly against its flysheet.

'Jackie?'

There was a sound of unzipping and Jackie's gaunt face poked out from the nylon den, eyelids flickering, evidently wasted on smack.

'Come in! Come in! Come into my wee palace Inspector Curzon!' Then she did one of her horse-throated, chesty cough laughs.

After looking around to check nobody was watching, Curzon stooped to climb inside.

'There's nothing hazardous in here now is there Jackie?'

'Don't panic!'

Poking his head in, he scanned the bare plastic ground sheet of the new smelling tent, before entering and sitting, legs crossed near the opening, with Jackie lying on her side up the west wing, resting her face on her left elbow, cheek in the cup of her hand.

'What the hell's all this about Jackie?'

'I went to Castlemilk just like you asked. I was in the pub there when some gadge came in selling tents for a tenner, so I thought: *there's no way I'm gonna miss my appointment if I camp on the spot.* I didn't want to risk whatever forfeit you'd no doubt got planned for me if I'd gouched out somewhere and failed to show.'

'Sensible girl.'

'It was a lovely night too. I was lying out on the grass thinking how I could just get into the outdoor lifestyle, maybe go hiking in the highlands, get off the heroin, be free of you – and then this bastern thunderstorm started! Fucking typical isn't it?'

'Aye, it is so.' Curzon shook some of the excess water from his hair with his fingers. 'Anyway, what have you got for me?'

At this point Jackie's eyelids began to flicker again and then close, causing Curzon to have to lean over and shake her by a scrawny shoulder blade. She jerked upright, opened her eyes as wide as a frog's and burst into a fit of giggles, then started rubbing the lapel of the detective's unbuttoned raincoat between her thumb and forefinger.

'You're after murderers aren't you, you Dirty- Rouge you!'

Then she started giggling again, head drooping so that Curzon had to hold her up by both sticklike shoulders.

'Aye, I'm after murderers,' he confessed impatiently. 'Now tell me what you know…or so help me God I'll…'

Jackie held an index finger to her mouth: 'Shush. There's no need to shout.' Then she began laughing again before registering the aggression in Curzon's eyes and trying to stop. 'No. No. Hold on. Here goes.' She took a deep breath and held both arms out in front of her, as if conducting a séance, until her fit of giggles finally subsided. 'The guy you're after is called Craig Hunter'

'Aha. Where is he?'

'He's stopping over in East Kilbride at a lad called Gaddafi's house, until the heat cools down, apparently. According to everyone in the Oasis Bar, he's popped the guy you found on the beach over a drugs debt.'

'Is that it?' Curzon exclaimed disappointedly.

''Is that it?'' Well, it's a damn site more than you've managed to get, otherwise he'd no' be at large and you'd no' be here…so where's my bloody heroin you old scoundrel you?'

As a fresh volley of thunder rumbled, Curzon produced another two wraps from his raincoat, which Jackie took and stuffed down the front of her tracksuit bottoms, into her knickers, before raising her eyebrows coquettishly.

'Why don't you hang around a wee while till the rain stops inspector? We'll call it another fifty quid?'

Although Curzon declined Jackie's offer without a moment's thought, even he felt a hint of shame at the contradiction between his fantasies and his reality. The previous night he'd literally shot his load imagining her on all fours on top of a grave slab, yet here he was with the opportunity to do it for real, in the rain, during a thunderstorm – and he was running away. Still, it might help at this point to inform you that DCI Patrick Curzon had never, ever enjoyed intimate contact with a woman, not even just a peck on the cheek. The bullying he'd suffered as a boy, along with his daily experience of the dark side of human nature in his job, had left him unable to trust people full stop, and so he kept everyone at a very long arm's length. Knowing this, one couldn't help but wonder what exactly went on during his visits to Nancy.

Chapter 7

Back at the station, Curzon begged a cooked breakfast in the canteen, which he ate in his office while his trousers and overcoat dried out over the radiator. At eight-thirty, Deegan and McKay arrived and, after ascertaining the real name of *Gaddafi*, from East Kilbride police station, they all went down to another metallic grey Ford Mondeo, which they drove through the incessant rain, followed by a riot van full of officers. Once they'd reached their target's address on a sprawling estate of grey, pebble-dashed houses, McKay walked round to the back of the property with two uniformed boys, while Curzon and Deegan knocked at the front, the other officers lying in wait at the side of the building. At first the occupants pretended no to be home until a short-haired, peroxide blonde girl in a pink Lacoste polo T-shirt popped her head out of an upstairs front window, asking what all the fuss was about and claiming to be alone. She stubbornly refused to open the door, much to the aggravation of everyone stuck outside in the deluge and, it was only when a couple of uniformed officers came from the side of the house carrying a battering ram that she eventually capitulated. It was obvious that she'd been biding time while the suspect concealed himself somewhere on the property, so it came as no surprise when a WPC located both Gaddafi – who really was the spitting image of the former Libyan leader – and Craig Hunter hiding behind the water tank in the attic, where they were arrested on suspicion of murder, as was the female householder.

On their return to the station, McKay interviewed Gaddafi and his girlfriend, while Curzon and Deegan interrogated Craig Hunter, the prime suspect. He was a pretty distinctive looking character with crew cut ginger hair, a ski ramp nose and slightly slanted eyes which contained chestnut brown pupils, dilated through a combination of sheer terror and recent cocaine inhalation.

Before starting to interview Hunter – who'd been stripped of his black Hugo boss T-shirt and matching Armani jeans and was now wearing a white paper suit – Curzon noted several shallow bite marks on each of his knuckles.

'What's with the knuckles son?'

'Eh?' Hunter looked down, stretched his fingers out and stared. 'Oh, right. I was lying on Gaddafi's sofa all last night waiting for you to come. Every time I heard a car door slamming shut outside or an engine running, my heart started beating so loudly that I actually couldn't hear what was going on, so I started biting my knuckles, coz it seemed to calm the thud down in my heart and my head.'

On hearing such an uninhibited, detailed outpouring, Curzon was anticipating an instant confession coming on, until:

'It wasn't me! I swear to God it wasn't me!'

'Then why were you so scared of us?'

'Because I was charging around on Saturday searching for Bobby…telling people that when I found him I was...'. Hunter looked down at the table top ashamedly. 'Telling people that I was gonna kill him.' He looked up again. 'It's just an unfortunate turn of phrase, you know.'

'Portentous even,' Deegan interjected.

'Eh?' the suspect exclaimed in ignorance.

'Never mind that now,' Curzon insisted. 'I just want to know why it was that you felt the need to say such a thing.'

Hunter put his elbows on the table, placed his head in his hands and sighed, before mumbling:

'Coz he's been screwing my woman.'

Curzon raised his eyebrows, as if shocked. 'He was a bit of a ladies' man then?'

Hunter looked up, suddenly animated, eager to impress his version of Bobby McQueen on Curzon.

'Oh aye, was he no'. Not only was he a good-looking guy but he had the patter, know what I mean?' Hunter gulped, tears welling up in his eyes. 'He was my best pal, the dirty, rotten bastard!'

Deegan handed him a Kleenex and, after wiping his eyes dry, the suspect continued.

'He was even banging the woman in charge of his probation course over at the new social-workers centre.' Then he started laughing. 'He reckoned she was into some right kinky stuff.'

Curzon remained inscrutable, but in truth his curiosity had been aroused properly for the first time so far during this case.

'Did you ever see this woman?' the DCI asked hopefully.

'Nah…he just told me about it.'

'We noticed that you were the last person to make a call to his phone. Could you tell us what that conversation was about?'

'I just wanted to know where he was.'

'So you could kill him?'

'No! For fuck's sake man! I told you, it was just words that I really wish I hadn't said now!' Hunter started scratching his ginger crew-cut hair. 'He told me he was at this party round at some posh house up the West End. So I went over there, but by the time I arrived he'd gone.'

'And you never saw him again?'

Hunter shook his head, then his lips started quivering and he broke down in tears.

Curzon decided this was a good place to adjourn proceedings, not least because he'd been struggling to supress a bowel movement throughout. Leaving Deegan to formally suspend the interrogation, he stood up tentatively, before shuffling out of the interview room, petrified that the hard stool which was already peeping from his sphincter might escape otherwise. Anybody who passed him in the corridor would have been convinced he'd slipped a disc, so slow and stiff were his steps. Eventually, after what had seemed an interminable journey, he reached a toilet and experienced the unparalleled relief of hearing his burden plonk in the water beneath him. Curzon always found this moment, directly after defecation, to be the most relaxing on earth and would often sit for up to ten minutes after, just letting his mind wander. The problem with this, though, was that his deposits positively reeked and so the delay between dispatch and flushing hardly helped matters, in fact, it merely allowed his steaming faeces to ferment and permeate the whole second floor of the police station, causing his disgusted colleagues to have to move about with their hands and jackets over their faces. Of course, nobody dared point this out to the vindictive inspector for fear of inspiring his wrath, and, anyway, the knowledge that he was causing discomfort to his fellow humans would only have pleased him.

It must be said that Curzon enjoyed an unhealthy fixation with his own shite, which a psychiatrist would probably attribute to his neglected childhood. His father had been constantly drunk, his mother always sedated, so toilet-training had never really taken place. Arguably, as a result, he'd never fully shed the anal stage of his development, which was why he liked to play mischievous games with his bodily waste now. Over the years he'd crouched on many a doorstep in order to deposit his meaty torpedoes of spite, with lawyers and gangsters being his preferred victims. He'd even broken into the home of one sadistic drug dealer called Steve Black, where he'd left a particularly nauseating specimen under a bed pillow, necessitating a visit from Rentokil in order to the find the source of the diabolical stench. When, finally, Black had been presented with the offending object, he'd become totally paranoid and never lived in that property again. Convinced he'd been targeted by a rival, he'd handed the stool to an associate on the police force, so that it could be DNA-tested by forensics. Of course, the molecules procured had no match on the national criminal database, thus eliminating anybody from the Glasgow underworld. So, just as Black's mind was put at rest, Curzon's had spun into a fever of justifiable panic. Not only was his DNA now on file, but it was damning evidence in an unsolved burglary. Every day since, for the past three years, he'd fretted about this. What if he were arrested somewhere out of his force's jurisdiction? Worse, what if there was another colleague as devious as him? All they'd have to do is pick up a cup he'd drunk from, harvest his DNA and then check it for a match on the off chance. Some nights he actually suffered a recurring nightmare in which all the malicious turds he'd dropped over the previous twenty years had been placed in evidence bags, labelled, dated and stored in freezers at a police facility somewhere in the city. In each dream, a bespectacled man in a white lab coat would remove a specimen from one of the fridges, which he then cross-referenced with DNA taken from Curzon after a drunk-driving incident. Half of the DCI's division were in attendance, standing behind the scientist in a crescent of bodies ten-deep, waiting with baited breath for him to confirm that they had indeed made a positive match. When he finally nodded in the affirmative, the whole room erupted with cheering and triumphant air-punching, while uniformed officers threw their hats in the air jubilantly. Horrible Curzon's reign was over.

Haunted by this spectre, Curzon had never, ever struck again and reserved his colonic calling card for the proper place.

Chapter 8

With Hunter back in his cell and nothing of note from either Gaddafi or his moll, Deegan drove Curzon over to a brand new social-work centre on the Southside. About the length of a small street and set back behind a parking area, the complex was a two-floored, brown-brick affair with a pavilion roof and blue plastic window frames. Curzon hated these sorts of purely functional, flexible buildings, with their landscaping and open spaces filled with mid-range cars. Indeed, he hated all the *new-builds* in Glasgow, not only in the city centre where they'd ruined the sandstone ambiance with titanium and glass or bright orange brick high-yield office blocks, but on the schemes too, where the grey, masculine and mean-looking post-war tenements were being replaced by energy-efficient, brick-built two-up two-downs with driveways and gardens. I mean who, he thought, would want to read a crime novel set in such a sterile setting?

On entering the foyer of the social work centre, the two detectives flashed their badges and asked the young receptionist if she could fetch the person in charge, which she very kindly did. While she was away, Curzon received a call from the lab confirming that the blood on the napkin from Frau Fuchs' back garden was indeed Bobby McQueen's. He was still digesting this information when Matilda Fuchs herself came out to greet them – in her capacity as head social worker. She was wearing the same clothes as the previous day, hair still tied back, only hanging here and there in wild, loose strands now, eyes looking very red as if she'd been doing a lot of crying. She and Curzon looked equally shocked to see one another, until the latter had recomposed himself enough to arrest the German, much to the bewilderment of Deegan.

Frau Fuchs sobbed all the way to the station, where Curzon let her stew for an hour in a cell before he began questioning, observed by his detective sergeant, in Interview Room number two.

'You lied to me Ms Fuchs.'

'I know. I'm sorry.'

'You will be.'

'I don't know anything about Bobby's death…really! It's just, I couldn't afford for people to find out about us…Oh God my career's over for good now.' She looked at Deegan as if expecting some sympathy. 'We'd been frolicking…frolicking? Is this the right word? Frolicking?' Deegan nodded. 'We'd been frolicking up at the centre in one of the store cupboards and once over in the Cathkin Braes…we had a picnic there.'

She looked from one to the other of her interrogators as if hoping that the romantic idea of a picnic might mitigate their view of her as some sort of slut. Unfortunately, though, it only reinforced any such thoughts, with Curzon and Deegan both imagining that this was where the *kinky* stuff must have occurred.

'Apart from that we never met outside the centre. I shouldn't have, but he's a good-looking boy….was a good-looking boy. That's my weakness: good-looking boys. It's why my husband left me.'

'Did either of you want the relationship to become more than *frolicking*?'

'No.' Frau Fuchs answered without hesitation, a little too fast for Curzon's liking, and her eyes seemed to wander guiltily after declaring it.

'So – and I want the truth this time – he was at your party wasn't he?'

'Yes. But we never had time to speak. I was busy attending to everybody and then, when I did go looking for him, he'd gone.'

'Did you invite him to the party?'

'No. Like I said, it would not be good for me to be seen with him. In fact, I was angry with him for turning up like that.'

'So how did he find out then? About the party I mean.'

'I don't know, it was either just coincidence or he maybe heard me talking to Anne about it…she's my colleague up at the centre.'

'By coincidence, do you mean he could have been invited by a friend of his, who was also a friend or a friend of a friend of yours, without even realising it was your party?'

'Yes. Yes, that's right.'

Frau Fuchs spoke as if the idea had never entered her head until now, but liked the sound of it because it helped her situation.

'OK. Ms Fuchs, we have acquired a paper napkin from your property with Bobby McQueen's blood on it. Can you provide any explanation as to how that blood might have got there?'

She shook her head, suddenly looking extremely worried.

'No. No, I'm sorry, I can't. You are frightening me now…I would like to speak to a lawyer please.'

'OK, OK. Just one last thing if you could. Was there anybody up at the probation centre who Bobby might have had issues with, anybody that might have had a reason to harm him?'

'No. Definitely not. He was very much liked by everybody. He was, how do you say – a bit of a lad?' Curzon smirked. 'Hold on a minute though.' Frau Fuchs pointed her right forefinger at her interrogators as if having a *eureka* moment. 'A carload of guys who had nothing to do with the centre turned up one day looking for him…didn't seem very friendly either.'

'Can you remember what they looked like? What sort of car they were driving?'

'Crew cuts, tracksuits, a white BMW convertible.'

'OK. Well, we'll speak to you again, just as soon as your legal representation arrives. In the meantime, feel free to enjoy the amenities in one of our *custody suites*.'

Outside in the corridor, Curzon turned to Deegan.

'I want her house turned upside down. Obviously we're looking for any serrated knives first and foremost, but cameras, phones and computers could be key I reckon…give us an idea of who exactly was at this party.'

Within two hours the mission had been accomplished, evidence bags full of knives from kitchen drawers were being analysed at the lab and over two hundred images of the party had been taken from a digital camera. Among these Curzon discovered that several featured Tommy Franklin: a recently retired, three times Scottish title-winning footballer who now managed lowly St. Clyde F.C. These photos were of particular interest because they showed Franklin manning the barbeque, where, of course, he'd have had instant access to a murder weapon. Curzon was just getting excited at the prospect of ruining a millionaire's day when something more gripping attracted his attention in the background of one of the snaps. It was Frau Fuchs' daughter – the same daughter who was supposed to be in Germany. When he mentioned this to Deegan, she explained that they'd also found flyers from the Ménage à Trance nightclub in her bedroom, flyers which could only have been handed out in the early hours of the morning before the party. This was significant because one of the few things they had learnt about the deceased was that he'd been a regular at this very trance music club.

Clutching the photo, Curzon stormed out of the office and jogged downstairs to Frau Fuchs' cell, where she was sat on a blue rubber mattress on a concrete bed, crying and moaning to her lawyer about the police searching her home and the violation of her privacy. They both looked up on hearing keys jangling in the door and were startled by the violent manner in which Curzon burst in, skimming the photo into the suspect's face.

'What's the story Frau Fuchs?!' he roared.

She fumbled the photograph which had fallen on her lap, then stared at it in evident horror.

'Did our local Casanova unwittingly have your precious little daughter at the Ménage à Trance nightclub last Friday night?'

Frau Fuchs looked away as if unable to entertain the thought. 'Please.'

'Then, on Saturday, he turned up at your party as invited by her. One way or another she found out about you two. There was a big argument. You stormed off to your room, had a bit of a cry. You don't know what happened after this point and because of that you've been protecting your daughter, because you're frightened that she may well be the murderer.'

Frau Fuchs' lawyer had been just as taken aback by Curzon's entrance as she had, and, as a consequence, took about thirty seconds to make his presence felt.

'DCI Curzon! I will not tolerate this aggressive and intimidating approach. What's more, neither will the law! My client has nothing to say and when and if she does, it will be in a proper, Criminal

Procedure Act-abiding environment!'

Curzon completely ignored him. 'Where is she Ms Fuchs? Where's your daughter?'

But Ms Fuchs, although shaking, remained silent, staring dead straight ahead at the chipped grey wall in front of her, irritating Curzon to such a degree that he slammed the cell door behind him on his way out.

Chapter 9

Now that he had to find the daughter, Curzon returned to Frau Fuchs' house and personally went through every detail of the nineteen-year-old's bedroom, until he found a red, leather-bound diary, its final entry made the day of the party, chronicling her kiss with a 'hottie' called Bobby the previous night at Ménage à Trance and describing how she couldn't wait to see him at her mother's barbeque. The fact that there'd been no entry since seemed to validate his hypothesis: that its owner, Monika Fuchs, had rushed away quite suddenly and unexpectedly in the wake of some tumultuous event. The other important thing he gleaned from the diary was the first name of her best friend, meaning that poor DC McKay would now have to draw up a shortlist of all the nineteen-year-olds in the city by the name of Lauren. Once the machine went into action, though, things moved remarkably fast and, by nine o'clock that evening Curzon and Deegan were stood on the landing outside Lauren Smith's apartment in Hillhead, badges in hand. They only had to knock once before a jovial girl with hazel-coloured curly hair answered the door, filling the stair with the trance music which was playing on the stereo behind her. She wasn't the least perturbed when they asked for Monika and didn't hesitate to ask them inside, where their quarry was sat on the sofa in the lotus position, drinking red wine. If anything she was even more attractive than her picture, because not only was her hair as blonde as lightening, but she had the most striking baby blue eyes that had to be engaged to be believed. When asked what she knew about Bobby McQueen's murder she looked genuinely nonplussed and claimed not to have spoken to her mother or seen any news or papers in the intervening period since Saturday night. Either way, Curzon was obliged to take her to the station, where he wasted no time in going to Frau Fuchs' cell to announce the fact triumphantly.

'So maybe you'd like to tell us the truth now, before she does?'

Frau Fuchs jumped from her rubber mattress and made a dash for the open cell door, where she was restrained by Curzon while shrieking down the corridor:

'Monika! Don't say anything! Don't say a word until you have a lawyer! Whatever you may think of me, don't go and ruin your life by speaking to these people!'

Not that Monika would have heard anything, because she was already sat in one of the interview rooms with DS Denise Deegan, ready to go. When Curzon arrived and took a seat, he slammed her red diary down on the table, causing her to experience the same harrowing sense of violation her mother had complained about earlier.

'We know you kissed Bobby in the early hours of Saturday morning. We also know that the last time anybody saw him alive was at your mother's party on Saturday night.'

'At least I'll never have to see him again.' Monika sniffled, trying to hold back the tears of frustration and anger she felt at being effectively kidnapped and having her private thoughts mulled over by middle-aged strangers. 'The very thought of him makes me feel sick,' she said, in a very soft and attractive, educated Scottish accent.

'Sick enough to kill?' Curzon asked abruptly.

Monika shook her head and turned to face Deegan for a moment, as if expecting her to understand what a man obviously couldn't.

'Because the way things are looking, Bobby was murdered round at your house.'

Monika shook her head again, lower lip hanging as if in disbelief.

'So, I take it you witnessed him leave the house in good health then?' Curzon continued.

'No, no I didn't actually see him leave.'

'Who else did he speak to at the party?'

'Nobody really.'

'Nobody really? He didn't speak to your mother then?'

'Oh yes, they were doing plenty of talking when I found them, if you know what I mean?' Monika raised her eyebrows. 'I still can't believe they were actually doing it in my bedroom.' She turned her head towards the wall, screwing her face up in disgust. 'But then nothing that woman does really shocks me anymore...she's a whore! That's why my dad left us. You know, she only does that social worker's job so she can get laid by rough young criminals. I honestly think she's systematically trying to fuck her way through every one of Glasgow's young offenders.'

Indeed, it had been a source of great puzzlement to Curzon as to how a social worker managed to afford a seven-hundred-thousand-pound townhouse. After further investigation, it transpired that Frau Fuchs' ex-husband had accumulated an estimated ten million pounds from his Silicon Glen-based electronics firm, at least fifty per cent of which had found its way into her bank account as part of their divorce settlement. Knowing this, it seemed highly probable that young Monika was right and that the social work centre was nothing more than a stud farm for her nymphomaniac mother. Frau Fuchs' anxieties about jeopardizing her job had had nothing to do with losing her livelihood, but everything to do with losing access to an environment which provided rich pickings for someone with her particular sexual proclivities: working class bad boys. In fact, Curzon had noted parallels between her distress at the prospect of losing her supply of young men and that of junkies he'd had in custody, when they think they're not going to get out of the cells in time for their next hit.

'So what did you do when you discovered them then? How did you react?'

Monika shrugged her shoulders self-consciously. 'Screamed, called my mother all the names under the sun, threw a perfume bottle at that horrible creep Bobby then ran out. I thought I was gonna get a slap, coz he chased after me.'

'Really?' Deegan interrupted, exaggerating her concern in an attempt to get Monika to gush information. 'My God, did he catch you?'

'No. I hid in the stairwell that goes down to our cellar and watched him run outside.'

'I thought you said you didn't see him leave?' Curzon interjected, retaking exclusive control of the interview again.

'He came back. I was upstairs, packing stuff into a backpack in my room and I heard his voice outside in the garden, right below my window.'

'What was he saying? Can you remember?'

'I didn't hear much because of that horrible modern jazz crap my mother and her cronies all listen to. But there was a brief moment when the music stopped and I heard him saying to someone, quite aggressively: *Remember me? Eh? Do you? Do you remember me?*'

'And was there a reply?'

'Don't know. The music resumed and I never heard another thing.'

Curzon decided they'd asked enough questions for the time being, but before terminating the interview he got Monika to look through the photos from the party, asking her to name any of the people he simply didn't like the look of, most notably a weedy, weasel-faced, middle-aged man with wispy fair hair, wearing a banana yellow and white Hawaiian shirt with chinos. This garishly-dressed character was helping out on the barbeque, next to Tommy Franklin, the ex-footballer.

'Oh that's Alistair.'

'What's he like?'

'Alistair? Oh, he's a lovely fella…it's a shame.'

'A shame? Why, what's up, is he ill? He looks ill.'

Monika afforded herself a little laugh. 'No, it's just that he's really, really liked my mum for years. He'll do anything for her, hence the reason he's operating the barbeque.'

'And your mother's not interested?'

'Not in that way, no. She's too busy screwing axe murderers to have time for someone normal like him. But he won't give up. No matter how many affairs my mother has, he's still always there, hanging about on the periphery of their crowd, following her around just in case she changes her mind. He's definitely totally in love with her, the poor fellow.'

Another angle had opened up now, which Curzon couldn't really pursue until ten o'clock the following morning, when he visited Alistair Meaks, the lovesick weasel, at his West End flower shop. Initially posing as just another customer, the policeman observed this nervy, weak-looking man smarming round elderly female customers with a trembling, inoffensive voice and even more shaky hands as he gathered the bouquets, which became almost invisible against the multi-coloured, short-sleeved shirt in a Picasso print he was wearing.

Eventually, after about twenty minutes of browsing the flora, Curzon was the only customer left in the shop.

'Hi there, can I help you sir?'

The fawning proprietor's palsied voice slithered tentatively up Curzon's spine and into his ear, exciting the very opposite effect to that of the innocuousness intended. *'Oh God, please let it be him,'* he thought to himself as he turned to face the weasel, whose eyes – of a weak piss-yellow – darted away before the detective could capture them with his own. On seeing Curzon's badge, the creature immediately turned his back and scurried to the door, putting the catch on and changing the OPEN sign to CLOSED, preventing his visitor from witnessing his initial facial reaction in the process. He seemed to hesitate a moment before turning back around, almost as if he were taking a deep breath and bracing himself, psyching himself up even for his big act. When he did finally turn to face Curzon again, he was sporting a nervous grin, of the please-don't-hit-me variety, which made the investigator want to do precisely that.

'How can I help you chief inspector?' he asked in his terminally servile manner, before disappearing behind the central display of flowers, so that Curzon really did feel as if he were conducting a conversation with some neurotic stoat.

'It's about Matilda Fuchs' party last Saturday night.'

Even more irritated now, Curzon raised his voice so that it would carry across the tiered display of foxgloves, tulips and red roses standing between them, all huddled together in their black plastic buckets of water.

The weasel re-emerged round the opposite, shop-counter end of the central display, clutching several dancing sunflowers.

'I thought as much,' he said solemnly. 'It's a terrible affair, not least for poor Matilda.'

His nervous grin had now given way to a priestly simper, trying to exude sympathy for everyone involved in the tragedy. It was so sickening in fact, that Curzon felt an urge to grab him by the scruff of his trembling, chicken neck and drown him in one of his buckets.

'Mr Meaks, you were in charge of the barbeque on the night in question, is that right?'

'Yes, yes I was?'

Like a piece in a kaleidoscope, Meaks' permanent smile changed character yet again, this time looking smug and self-congratulatory, as if to say: *yes, I help people all the time, it's what I do, I'm a really nice guy.'*

'Can you tell me what you recollect about that night? Anything that might be of relevance to the case. Anything about anyone, even something little like somebody being in an unusual mood, maybe?'

'Yes, yes I can actually. It was just past ten o'clock – I know that coz dusk was starting to fall – when this young hoodlum I'd never seen before came swaggering into the garden, crew cut hair, jeans, navy blue T-shirt, football tattoo on his forearm. He walked straight past us and up on to the lawn, then washed his face in the birdbath…I suppose that counts as unusual, doesn't it?'

Curzon nodded. 'You said *us*? Who else was there?'

'It was just me and Tommy out there at the time cooking up the rest of the venison burgers.'

'Tommy?' Curzon inquired disingenuously.

'Yes, yes, Tommy Franklin, the footballer? Great guy…we're great friends,' Meaks gloated nauseatingly. 'Anyway, while this character was doing his *ablutions,* Tommy made a sharp exit, before he was recognized and no doubt harassed about football for the next three hours, which happens a lot to the poor fellow when he bumps into these morons with nothing else in their lives except *the match*.' Meaks rolled his eyes exasperatedly before continuing. 'So, muggins here was left alone with this individual. I was a bit on edge, coz I'd never seen him before and, at the risk of sounding snobby, he didn't really belong…if you get my drift?'

As somebody who'd never belonged himself and had been excluded as a child simply because of circumstances beyond his control, Curzon knew exactly what the weasel meant and detested him for it.

'Once he'd finished his wash, sure as God made little green apples, he came down to me at the barbeque, all familiar and matey and domineering like these lot from the schemes usually are: *Eh 'pal', chuck us one of them there burgers 'pal' will you 'pal'?'* So, I reluctantly stuffed one in a bun and handed it to the guy, hoping he'd be on his way, but it only encouraged him, and I couldn't slip off coz the barbeque kit would have probably been gone by the time I'd got back!' Meaks giggled self-consciously. 'Anyway, once he'd wolfed his food down, in about two seconds flat, he began banging on about what a *top guy* I was and what a *great burger* I cooked, then started rummaging in his pockets until he found a little cellophane-wrapped lump of cannabis and thrust it into my hand. In the process he accidently dropped a couple of wraps of what looked like harder stuff on the floor. I was just about to point this out when Matilda appeared, looking pretty damned angry. She shouted at him: *What are you doing here?* At first I assumed she was vexed because some passing stranger had gate-crashed her party, so when she turned to go back into the house and he followed her, I thought I'd better tag along to make sure everything was alright.'

'Go on.'

'To my shock it seemed they were already acquainted, because he followed Matilda upstairs to young Monika's room and shut the door behind him. I was trying to hear what was going on, when Monika herself came out from the bathroom, so I went in after her, as if that's what I'd been waiting for.'

'So how long would you say you spent in the bathroom?'

Alistair twitched. 'Sorry?' Then he turned his head slightly to one side, as if by putting his ear directly in the line of Curzon's words he would hear them better.

'How long, roughly, were you in the bathroom for?'

'Erm…it's difficult to say isn't it, I mean how long does anybody stay in a bathroom?'

'Long enough to roll and smoke your gift of cannabis perhaps? Or snort some of that cocaine the lad had dropped on the floor?' Curzon smiled, attempting to disarm Meaks, but our florist started to panic all the more.

'No, no, I didn't do either…I chucked the cannabis straight in the trash can, left the other stuff on the floor where it was…I mean I don't do drugs…never have.'

'OK, OK.' Curzon couldn't help himself from laughing out loud, so hysterical was Meaks' flap. 'So when you left the bathroom, what then? Did you witness anything of note?'

Meaks shook his head. 'No, the guy had gone by the time I'd come out and I found Matilda in her study crying.'

'About what?'

'She just said it was mother and daughter stuff.'

'So what did you do then, go back out to your barbeque or …?'

'I sat with her for half an hour or more first. By the time I got back out Tommy was packing everything up.'

Curzon nodded, eyes squinting in thought. 'OK Mr Meaks, thank you very much for your assistance…sorry to have inconvenienced you.'

'It's no problem, I'm always happy to help.'

Of course, Meaks said this in an über-obsequious way.

Before Curzon reached the door he turned around again and did his little imitation of American TV detective, Columbo, as much for his own amusement as its invaluable psychological impact on the suspect.

'Just one more thing Mr Meaks.'

From his inside, suit jacket pocket, Curzon produced a photograph taken of the barbeque area during the party, featuring Meaks cutting hotdog buns with a hitherto missing breadknife.

'You wouldn't happen to know the origins or present whereabouts of this particular breadknife would you?'

Meaks jerked backwards, furrowing his brow in an ostentatious display of puzzlement, before taking the photo from the detective's hand.

'The knife's from Matilda's kitchen,' he said, cautiously.

'Well it's not there now,' insisted Curzon.

Meaks immediately understood the implication.

'Maybe Tommy inadvertently took it with the rest of his stuff.'

'The barbeque equipment was Tommy's?'

'Yes, a lot of it,' Meaks said emphatically, leaving no doubt that neither the origin of the knife nor its destiny had anything to do with him, though Curzon could see that his mind was now working overtime, which was how he liked to leave his victims…I mean suspects.

'And what about this blue tarpaulin here?' Curzon pointed to the bottom right-hand corner of the picture, which was still in Meaks' hand. On the floor, where the front of the brick barbeque met the next-door neighbour's stone boundary wall at a right angle, there was a rucked-up piece of old tarpaulin, which had probably been used to protect the DIY construction from the elements, when not in use. 'Do we have any idea where that went? Only it's not there now either.'

Meaks put his free hand to his mouth and dragged his open thumb and forefinger down his chin.

'I never even noticed it at the time.'

Curzon retrieved the photograph. 'Thank you again Mr Meaks.'

Meaks lunged nervously towards the door, his shaking fingers fumbling the catch, the sunflowers in his left hand writhing like some botanical Houdini trying to escape the straightjacket of his quaking grasp.

Chapter 11

During the fifteen-minute train journey to Tommy Franklin's house in Bearsden, Curzon reflected on his conversation with the weasel. Not only had he been photographed holding a possible murder weapon, right next to where the deceased's blood was discovered, but he'd admitted to being alone with the victim, providing ample time to carry out the crime. And even if he'd not done it during that particular window of opportunity, Curzon thought, then what about the period he claimed to have spent in the bathroom, or the rough estimate of half an hour consoling Frau Fuchs? Within either of these unverifiable time spaces he could quite easily have committed murder. Most crucially, though, for Curzon, was the fact that Meaks had a plausible motive: jealousy. Not to mention that he could have slain Bobby McQueen out of some chivalric act of duty towards Frau Fuchs, willing to punish anyone who caused her sadness or injury, like a brother or father might for a dishonoured sister or daughter. Furthermore, he'd been extremely edgy during Curzon's visit, his reactions and responses seeming inauthentic. However, Curzon reckoned Meaks was probably insincere on a full-time basis, phoniness being a functional prerequisite for shopkeepers. Also, the florist had been genuinely shocked to learn that the barbeque breadknife might be the murder weapon, a theory which propelled him to deflect suspicion away from himself by alerting Curzon to the existence of another suspect. Either way, he'd brought Tommy Franklin well and truly into the frame, much to the detective's delight.

Surrounded by mature Sycamore trees, Franklin's house was a six-bedroom, sandstone villa, set back behind baroque security gates and a seven-foot privet hedge. On the gravel drive, three recently-hosed vehicles gleamed in the summer sunshine: a sapphire-blue Porsche, a black Range Rover and a nineteen-fifty-seven, vintage silver Bentley, all sporting personalised number plates. It came as no surprise when Curzon was refused admission over the intercom and he knew that he shouldn't interpret any guilt from this, because all professional footballers had been drilled to contact their clubs under such circumstances, who in turn rang their lawyers before anybody made any statements to anyone. So, Curzon threatened Franklin with a warrant, saying that he could get one within the hour, then went round to the rear of the property, scaled the seven-foot stone wall and dropped down into the wooded margins of the star's garden. Here, among flowering elder trees and rhododendron bushes, he crunched his way through the undergrowth, snagging himself repeatedly on raspberry bushes as he progressed, cursing all the way.

There was no practical purpose to this unorthodox course of action, other than Curzon's stubborn refusal to be repelled from anywhere he wanted to enter. Under no circumstances was he going to be told what to do or where to go by anybody. One way or another, he was adamant he was going to get into that house, if only to spook the owner, whose rudeness and inhospitality needed redressing.

As Curzon reached the edge of the long, manicured lawn, he spied a French window open on the terrace, about thirty yards up ahead. He was just about to sprint towards it when Franklin burst out carrying what looked like two encyclopaedias under his right arm and a spade in his left hand. The detective stepped sideways into a large rhododendron bush, from where he watched the six-foot-three, blonde-haired footballer march down the lawn towards him, so pinpointedly that he assumed he'd been rumbled. It was only as the square-jawed athlete got closer, the sheer hulk-like heft of his muscular body threatening to tear the black T-shirt and blue jeans he was wearing, that Curzon suddenly started to worry about being murdered as an intruder. After all, if Franklin was already a vicious knife killer, what was to stop him using a spade to bludgeon a prowler on his own property?

With Franklin so close you could see the steely blue of his eyes, Curzon wanted to blow his cover and run. But he found himself frozen to the spot, holding his breath, tensing his body, heart thumping so fast and loud he was sure that the suspect could hear it too. Mercifully, the footballer brushed straight past the bush and out of view, leaving Curzon to rely on sound, as attempting to turn and watch would have caused too much noise from the cracking sticks beneath his feet. He then heard several stabs of a spade, interspersed with the shovelling of earth, before Franklin brushed past the bush again on his way back to the house, minus the encyclopaedias, gardening implement in hand.

As soon as Franklin was safely back in his house, the French door locked behind him, Curzon climbed out of the rhododendron and located a square of disturbed earth amongst the bushes in the lea of the wall, which he excavated by toe-poking it with his brown suede shoe. He'd been expecting to find accounts, evidence perhaps of tax fraud or embezzlement from the football club Franklin was now managing. But it turned out that the buried objects weren't books at all but black, leather-bound photograph albums, stacked one on top of the other. Crouching on his haunches, Curzon picked one up and rested it upon his knees to open. It was certainly not what he'd been expecting. The first page contained a large photograph of a buff Franklin on an East Asian beach, wearing a vest, speedo pants and flip-flops, his arm around a local teenage boy in swimming trunks. Except for the occasional picture of the ex-footballer reclining with a beer, the subsequent photos were pretty much the same, only the teenage boys were different each time. On some he had two boys, one on either side, and in another particularly creepy snap he was lying on a bed in what looked like some kind of beach hut, wearing only trunks, with an arm around another semi-naked young man. Even to someone as cynical as Curzon, viewing these images felt like swallowing condemned meat and, after closing the album, he remained on his haunches for a good minute, cogitating on what implications this might have on his case, before putting both books under his right arm and snapping and cracking his way back through the vegetation and climbing out of the garden.

As Curzon boarded the train back to town he got a call from an anxious sounding Deegan.

'Boss, we've got some bad news.'

'Go on?'

'The blood on the paper napkin? It might not have been spilled round at Ms Fuchs'.

'How so?'

'We've just had a taxi driver walk into the station, recognises Bobby McQueen as a fare he picked up on Saturday night outside The Goose on Union Street at around ten. Apparently, he had a small nose bleed and was holding a napkin against it. McKay's been down to view their CCTV from the weekend, and sure enough, he's on there having a tussle with a group of guys, one of their number being, guess who?'

'Craig Hunter?

'Got it in one. Not only that, but we've also got CCTV footage of the crew in the BMW convertible that Ms Fuchs told us about, from a filling station forecourt in Rutherglen. Again, it's Craig Hunter and...'

'And who?'

'Our old friend Stevie Black.'

Now aged fifty, Steve Black was an infamous East End drug dealer who never handled his merchandise and always got the street dealers he employed – called his *dustmen* – to personally inflict retribution on any bad debtors they'd supplied to, otherwise they'd have to foot the bill themselves, one way or another. On the surface, it was beginning to look like Bobby McQueen had maybe run up debts to his mate Craig Hunter, who'd been coerced to enact punishment by his boss, Black, who was, above all else, a misanthropic sadist who would derive great pleasure from seeing a man kill his own son. Indeed, any atom of humanity that Black may once have possessed had been reserved for Comet, his prize-winning racing pigeon, which was now stuffed and mounted and occupying pride of place on DCI Curzon's mantelpiece.

'That lying wee bastard!' Curzon shouted angrily, unnerving his fellow train passengers in the process.

'Indeed. And what's more, from the little the good folk of Castlemilk are telling us, it seems the cuckolding girlfriend is a fiction of Hunter's imagination too. Not one person has ever seen him with a partner.'

'Sneaky wee shite,' Curzon snarled.

'What are the odds that after the fight was split up by the bouncers, Craig Hunter and co followed Bobby McQueen to Ms Fuchs', then waited for him outside and finished him off on his way home? I wouldn't be surprised if Bobby had taken one of the knives from the barbeque himself, for self-defence, only to have it turned against him during the melee.'

'These cases usually end up being pretty obvious, but you've got to maintain an open mind and, more importantly, what I've always taught you: try and keep the investigation open as long as possible. Remember, it's an opportunity to dig precious dirt we would never get otherwise.'

Curzon was ambivalent about this piece of news because, if it turned out that Craig Hunter was the killer, then it meant that his more ingenious theories couldn't be realized. Yes, most murders were quite boring, open-and-shut cases, an obvious culprit closely associated with the victim. But this one had started to look more interesting, like something out of one of the Chandler novels he'd read as a kid. Now, though, it seemed that the blood-stained napkin round at Frau Fuchs' back garden had probably fallen from Bobby's pocket while he'd been rummaging for the cannabis he'd given to Alistair Meaks. Also, the need to rinse the blood from his face after having had his nose busted would account for the bird bath swill, as described by the florist.

On the journey back into town, Curzon reviewed the investigation in his head. Not only did Craig Hunter have a motive, but he also freely admitted that he'd been hunting McQueen down and telling folk that he was going to kill him. As for the other, now discredited prong of the inquiry, revolving around Frau Fuchs' barbeque, Curzon recapped on the actual evidence all the same. For starters, Frau Fuchs had become entangled in a love triangle which involved Bobby McQueen and her own daughter, thus providing the quintessential murder motive. A feeling of scorn, betrayal and jealousy might have induced a fit of rage, resulting in her snatching a bread knife from the barbeque and finishing the philanderer off. Her loyal lapdog, Alistair *the weasel* Meaks, may well have assisted in disposing of the body. But it was unlikely, because Frau Fuchs' response on being told of Bobby's death was one of absolute, genuine shock. On the other hand, the weasel may have committed the murder himself, motivated by either envy or a sense of loyalty towards Frau Fuchs. And, of course, there'd always been a strong chance that Monika, the daughter, had committed the deadly deed for much the same reasons as her mother, hence Frau Fuchs' determination to protect her. As for Franklin, well, he'd been a real dark horse who'd aroused Curzon's detective instincts, but it looked like they'd come to nothing now that all fingers were pointing at Craig Hunter. The only thing which still bugged Curzon about the footballer, apart from him probably being a paedophile, was the fact that in some of the East Asian photographs he was smoking a cigarette, belying the clean-living, fitness freak image portrayed by his sponsors. Not only that, but as a youth-player such a vice would have made him unattractive to clubs and almost definitely scuppered his career, meaning that he'd probably learned to indulge his penchant for nicotine in secret. This might explain why the only other place Curzon had ever seen one of the particularly distinctive, shiny gold-papered cigarette butts from the photos, was in the area beneath Frau Fuchs' front-door steps.

Chapter 12

By the time Curzon got back to the station, Tommy Franklin's lawyer, Fergus Baxter, had already phoned one of the assistant chief constables. He'd demanded that the inspector be withdrawn from the case because he was harassing his client – against whom there was no evidence – simply on the grounds that the 'poor man' was being represented by him. He claimed that Curzon was being childishly unprofessional and that he held a vendetta over the Maker case, even going so far as to recommend psychological counselling, before threatening to write a letter to the Police Complaints Commissioner.

When people as esteemed and dangerous as Fergus Baxter made complaints on behalf of rich, national icons, adored by the public and feted by the establishment, senior policemen had to take notice and make sure everything was done by the book. Ideally, they preferred things to be conducted as informally as possible, which was why the assistant chief constable had arranged an appointment for Curzon at Baxter's West George Street chambers in the city centre, later that afternoon. He'd told Curzon's superintendent to stress to his inspector that, once he'd spoken with Franklin and Baxter, if there was still no overwhelming evidence, he should discontinue this particular 'fruitless and unnecessarily invidious line of inquiry'. As far as the chief was concerned, properly investigating the murder of one petty criminal from a scheme really wasn't worth a running battle with the various powerful interest groups, which would distract him from the general fight against crime and eventually ensure his premature departure from the post.

In the meantime, Craig Hunter was already being re-interrogated by DS Deegan and DC McKay in interview suite number two, where he was tearfully pleading his innocence again.

'You've got to believe me! I didn't do it!'

As Curzon entered, he leapt up from his chair and ran round the table, paper suit rustling, arms stretched imploringly towards the chief inspector.

'Tell them! You know! I know you know that I didn't do it! Please! Tell them!'

Curzon stood in silence, staring deep into Hunter's eyes, trying to work out if he were telling the truth, but you could never really be sure. He'd seen this type of histrionics countless times from murder suspects, often from the innocent, but occasionally from the guilty too, as the true horror of a possible life sentence set in. Sometimes though, they just couldn't confront the magnitude of what they'd done and so succumbed to temporary denial, so deep that they genuinely believed themselves to be guiltless, even though they weren't.

Curzon ushered Hunter back into his seat but remained standing himself.

'So why did you do it? Why did you lie to me?'

Hunter shook his head, trembling lips curled and contorted. 'I'm sorry, but I was always going to be prime suspect and that video evidence from The Goose would've sunk me...is gonna sink me!...Oh God!'

The suspect buried his ginger head in his hands, his whole body shaking violently now.

Fortunately for Curzon, Hunter had never asked for any legal representation. If there had been an advocate present he would almost certainly have demanded the termination of this interview and requested a doctor, such was the magnitude of the breakdown the suspect was obviously undergoing. Curzon was more than aware of Hunter's vulnerability, but was quite happy to exploit the situation and completely break the man if necessary.

'I'm not on about The Goose. You didn't lie to me about The Goose, you just never told me. You lied to me about Bobby screwing your imaginary girlfriend. Why?'

'Because it was less incriminating.'

'Less incriminating than what?'

Hunter pointed at the tape machine and did the throat-slitting gesture with his hand and whispered: 'Turn the tape off and I'll tell you everything.'

Impressed at the way his suspect had suddenly recomposed himself, Curzon nodded respectfully and pressed the stop button on the machine.

'And I want it to be just you and me,' Hunter insisted.

Curzon nodded again, this time in a sarcastically deferential manner, while Deegan and McKay got up and left of their own accords, sparing themselves the indignity of having to be told at the behest of a petty criminal, possibly a murderer.

'OK then, from the beginning,' the D.C.I prompted Hunter impatiently, 'and don't omit a thing now, coz if you do I'll find out and I'll make sure you take the rap for this, whether you did it or not.'

'Don't worry, this time I'm gonna tell you everything, coz it's really starting to freak me out.'

Having taken a seat, Curzon reclined in his chair and spun a horizontal forefinger round like a fishing reel, gesturing that he wanted Hunter to speed things up.

'I was having coke laid onto me, which I was then laying onto other people, one of whom was Bobby. But he was a useless dealer. What he didn't put up his own nose he was giving away to all his women. He owed me two grand in the end, so I told him that was me and him finished as far as business went. One way or another I'd have to make sure my man got his money, but two grand's not that hard to make up so long as you cut your powder accordingly.'

'But you were pretty angry with him I'd imagine. Christ, I know I'd be.'

'I was pissed off, yes, but that's not the half of it.'

'Go on?'

'Every two weeks someone drops a kilo of coke at a secret place only me and Bobby knew about, then I go and pick it up. Three weeks ago, I turned up on drop day, only when I got there it had gone.'

'So, naturally you assumed Bobby had taken it.'

'Well, who else could have?'

'You could have been followed the time before. Somebody could have stumbled upon it by chance. The dropper might not even have dropped it there in the first place, kept the gear and left you to carry the can…it happens, believe me.'

'Aye, that crossed my mind, until I was told that Bobby was out in town on student night throwing the stuff around like confetti. The queue for the toilets started in the middle of the dancefloor down at Ménage, so I heard.' Hunter sighed. 'On Saturday morning I waited at the end of the street for him to come out from his parent's house, then followed him into the construction site opposite, until he stopped at a dumper truck and removed the remainder of my gear from under the seat where he'd hidden it.'

'What did you do?'

'I steamed into the fucker there and then. Bobby's a lot harder than me but he was taken by surprise. He knew I had right on my side and that made the difference, I think. Fortunately I got hold of what was left, about half a kilo, but there was no way I could replace the other half out of my own pocket…we're talking about twenty grand! So I went and explained to my man that half the gear had been stolen before I'd even got it. Can't believe I said half, I should have just said none of it was there in the first place, but I was in a bit of a panicky state, know what I mean? To make matters worse my man already knew Bobby had been flashing the gear around, coz one of his other dustmen told him that they had competition.'

'What did he say?'

'He said that the money was my responsibility and that if I could get it to him on the usual payday it was none of his business. If not, then I could pay him back in instalments from my earnings thereon. In other words, I'd be dealing for him for nothing until it was recouped. At first I thought we'd got off lightly, until he said that he couldn't afford to have people thinking that any of his dealers were soft, and that if I didn't get the money to him at the usual time, then I'd personally have to slash Bobby across the face.'

'Phew,' Curzon whistled.

'I was caught between a rock and a hard place. The only thing I could do was tell Bobby to get out of Glasgow before the two weeks were up. I mean, I was gonna have to pay the cash back either way, so that seemed like the best solution for everyone. I even saw him off at Buchanan Street bus station. He was hugging me, telling me he was sorry, that he loved me and that he was going down to London to work and that he'd get the money back to me, blah, blah, blah.' Hunter threw his arms up into the air to express his exasperation. 'Three weeks later and the prick's back...only attending his bloody probation meeting! He just couldn't keep away from that woman over there.' Sighing, he blew his cheeks out, then took a deep breath before continuing. 'Well, my man knows Bobby's back in town straight away and he's round my house in his motor with his crew, telling me to get my arse into the car. When we get up to the probation centre he hands me a craft knife and says: 'Now do it, coz if you don't do him, then I'm gonna have to do you.' Thankfully, Bobby must have spotted us, coz he managed to get out the back through a window or something. But by Saturday evening he'd been spotted out on the razzle and my man was beeping outside the house again. Anyway, we drove round the city centre, from pub to pub, and I had to go into each one chaperoned by two of his gimps, so they could make sure I carried my *assignment* through. I was telling anyone who knew Bobby that he was a dead man if I found him, not because I meant it, but because I was trying to please these heavies over my shoulder. Also, I thought, the more word got round, the less likely it was that we'd find him. Unfortunately, though, after about an hour traipsing about, we discovered him in The Goose. The rest you've seen for yourself on the tape.'

'I've heard about it...but you didn't do it?'

'I know, I punched him in the face instead and then deliberately dropped the knife in the scuffle.'

'I understand the bouncers intervened? What happened then?'

'We scarpered back to where the car had been parked, but my man had already gone.'

'No surprise there, Mr Black won't want to be implicated in any way?'

'Who?' Hunter made a pathetic display of mock ignorance.

'Don't panic. We already know who your *man* is, and we won't be mentioning you to him. We won't even be questioning the guy, there's no point.' Curzon was still reclining in his chair. 'So what happened next?'

Hunter shook his head before continuing.

'Black's men headed off their own way and I walked up through the town to clear my head, ended up on the Art School steps. That's when I decided to give Bobby a call.'

'Yes, that's something that's been bugging me. Bearing in mind that you'd just attacked him with a gang, while brandishing a craft knife, I'm intrigued to know how this conversation went. I mean, why on earth would he want to tell you where he was?'

'He knew why I did what I did and that I'd deliberately dropped the knife. I only punched him in the nose so as to avoid slashing him across the face.' Hunter opened his arms wide at either side in an appeal to Curzon's reason. 'But you're quite right, he probably wasn't taking any chances and that's why he'd gone by the time I reached the party up the West End. For all he knew, Black's crew were standing right behind me while I made the call.'

Curzon smiled to himself at the way Hunter had dropped his guard and was now completely unaware that he was name-dropping lethal gangsters.

'You do realize that the prosecution's gonna eat you for breakfast if that's your defence, don't you?' the DCI cautioned.

The more Hunter had got his story off his chest, the higher his spirits seemed to have climbed, but now, on hearing Curzon's latest grim statement, he collapsed into a trough of despondency again.

'Oh no, I knew you wouldn't believe me. Oh god. I'm not gonna see the outside world again am I? I'll be the talk of Castlemilk for a week and then nobody will even remember me.'

These last two words – the same words Monika Fuchs had heard the deceased utter to someone beneath her bedroom window – reverberated in Curzon's head like an echo of an echo of an echo. 'Remember me. Remember me. Remember me. Remember me.' With those words, a lot of vague fragments that had been swirling round in his mind for the past twenty-four hours suddenly coalesced. Until this moment they'd merely been feelings that he'd been unable to articulate even into thoughts, but now they were as instantly intelligible as his own name printed on a piece of white paper. It was like one of those instants when you've been searching for your car key, only to discover that it's already in your hand, and has been all the time.

Without any explanation, Curzon suddenly leapt up from his chair and darted out of the interview room, much to the consternation of Hunter.

Chapter 13

Having driven at high speed, Curzon skidded up outside the players' entrance at St. Clyde F.C, where he burst through the main double doors and marched through the reception area, before marauding round narrow corridors, popping his head into empty rooms with an irate secretary in his wake. After he'd held his ID badge backwards over his right shoulder she scampered back to her desk, leaving him, finally, to locate Frank Magivery – the first team coach – who was enjoying a sauna. On seeing the policeman, his previously contented, chiselled face contorted into a glower.

'And there was me thinking it was the wee senorita that does our physio.' He sighed resignedly. 'I'll be with you in five.'

Frank Magivery was a notoriously bad gambler. So bad in fact, that back in the Nineties he'd run up a debt of twenty grand to a local hood, who wanted him to start sabotaging the St. Clyde team for betting purposes, or else get thrown from the roof of the thirty-storey, Red Road flats. Not only was Magivery a gambler, but a regular visitor to the city's higher-quality brothels, where he'd enjoyed some of the girls provided by Curzon's friend, Nancy Nixon. After a demoralising loss at the roulette table, a few glasses of champagne, a bubble bath and a baby-oil massage at the long, manicured fingers of a seasoned, professional sex worker, it's easy for a man to drop his guard. This is what happened to Magivery the night he told the Ukrainian lass he'd just screwed all about his predicament with the Glasgow underworld. Naturally, she relayed the story back to Nancy, who told Curzon the next time he popped round to her Park Circus townhouse. So, now Magivery had to deliberately coach his football team to lose every few weeks, while at the same time keeping Curzon informed of any dressing room gossip that the police might be interested in, which was more often and of a more serious nature than you might at first think.

While the coach made himself decent, Curzon walked down the players' tunnel and out onto the spongy pitch, his feet sinking an inch into the turf with every step, before he stopped halfway towards the centre circle and surveyed the empty stadium. Imagining all the thousands of bawling humans that had congregated here since 1875, his permanent sneer intensified. To a cynical loner like Curzon, anything played by teams and enjoyed by crowds was positively repulsive, the equivalent of silver stakes and garlic to a vampire. Truth is, he detested every football player and every fan equally and was adamant that all professional sport was a fix.

Wearing a yellow club tracksuit, fifty-year-old Magivery, who was an athletic six foot-two with a good head of greying hair, came out onto the pitch to meet the detective.

'What can we do for you then Paddy?'

'It's nothing and everything really, Frank. I was just wondering if you remembered a young guy called Bobby McQueen? He was one of your apprentices here if I'm not mistaken?'

'Wasn't he just…cracking wee centre forward. By rights he should be getting ready for pre-season with Rangers or Celtic, but instead he's in the morgue.'

'You've heard then?'

'Aye.'

'Could you give me an idea of what his time was like here…what exactly were the circumstances of his departure?'

'He was a good kid, bit mouthy like, but aren't they all these days.' Magivery shrugged his shoulders. 'He was as much a definite for the big time as I've ever seen, then he got collared stealing stuff out of the first team dressing room while they were training. I did everything I could to keep him here, but our new star signing at the time, our present manager Mr *Tommy Franklin*, insisted that it was either Bobby or him. The chairman was well and truly coiled up Franklin's arse, so the young guy was finished. I couldn't understand it, coz Franklin was on his last legs and costing us money, whereas Bobby was just starting out and would most probably have made us a few quid. Still, I suppose the chairman didn't want to jeopardize his sea fishing jaunts on Franklin's wee yacht.'

'Franklin owns a boat?' Curzon exclaimed, almost with elation.

'Oh aye, he's got it moored on the Yacht Haven down at Largs.'

The detective started nodding his head approvingly, as if Magivery was confirming things that he already instinctively knew.

'Is there anything about Franklin as a character that I should know about?'

'Well, between ourselves, I can't stand the prick. I nearly punched him for what he did to that laddie.'

'So what happened exactly? Was it Franklin's stuff Bobby got caught stealing?'

'I don't know. Franklin just reckoned he'd walked into the dressing room and caught the young guy going through players' pockets. When the lad turned up for training next morning, he was refused admission onto the premises and told by security that he was banned from the club. He accosted me in the staff parking area later that afternoon, in tears he was, swearing he didn't have a clue what Franklin was going on about. I felt sorry for the kid and was gonna have another go at getting him reinstated, but then the next day we got reports back that he was going around telling ridiculous tales about Tommy Franklin having made a sexual pass at him.' Magivery shrugged his shoulders again. 'We couldn't have him back after that.'

Curzon extended his right arm directly in front of him and pointed his forefinger so that it was within an inch of Magivery's nose.

'You might be a bloody awful football trainer Magivery, but you're a Champions League snitch.'

And with that he marched off, leaving the bemused and insulted coach turning to watch him disappear down the whitewashed tunnel, no doubt wishing him a fatal injury.

Chapter 14

Curzon drove to the city centre and parked up in front of Fergus Baxter's plush West George Street chambers. Before entering, he stopped on the steps to ring Deegan and McKay, telling them to get over there as fast as possible in a detainment vehicle and to wait outside. In the meantime, he was greeted by the lawyer's sexy, bespectacled secretary, brown hair tied back in a bun, an ample bosom barely contained beneath a white silk blouse. As she led him to her master, high heels clicking, he admired the pert derriere, shrink-wrapped in a black, pinstriped pencil skirt, while congratulating himself for having found that night's wanking material.

Wearing his trademark green and brown tartan suit, the ginger goateed legal eagle stood up from behind his shiny oak desk to greet Curzon with a sickly smile, though spared him the hypocrisy of offering his hand to shake. Meanwhile, Tommy Franklin sat with his chair side-on to the desk, powerless-looking, like a naughty schoolboy in the head teacher's office, a sight completely at odds with the bossy centre forward who'd graced Sportscene every Saturday night for fifteen years, barking at referees and punching his clenched fist at opposing supporters whenever he'd been victorious.

'I trust this is about the murder of Robert McQueen?' Baxter said, rolling every 'R' to maximum, pompous effect. 'My client has given me a full account of his movements from the time the deceased went missing and until his body was found, and I can assure you, as an officer of the law who has been practising for over thirty years, that he has no case to answer.'

Baxter dropped his sickly, goading grin on Curzon again, before reading out a short, drafted statement on Franklin's behalf:

'My client wishes to help the Glasgow Police with their inquiries in whatever way he can. However, he is also mindful not to incriminate himself. Last Saturday night he attended a party at the home of Ms Matilda Fuchs in Westbourne Gardens, Glasgow, where he spent the entire evening cooking food on a barbeque on the back lawn. Once he'd finished doing this and had packed his equipment away it was nearly midnight, by which time he was quite understandably tired and so returned home to sleep until nine o'clock the following morning. Furthermore, my client knows of no incident or information that can have any relevance to Glasgow Police's Inquiry and wishes to exercise his right to say nothing further on the matter.'

Mouth shut, Baxter puffed his cheeks out proudly and smiled, so that he resembled a smug little birthday boy with a mouth full of cake. Behind this superficial contentment, though, were harmful eyes, dilated with rage and vengeance over the crank call to his advocate in court the previous Friday, which he knew, full well, had been orchestrated by Curzon. If it could have been possible for Baxter to compete any harder against the policeman, then now was the time, and the detective knew that merely providing evidence would not be enough to defeat this wily old tartan fox. In fact, by the look of determined aggression behind the affected smile, Curzon was pretty sure that Baxter was willing to drop however many other balls he may have been juggling, just to keep a tight grip on this one – even if the client were to quite blatantly confide his guilt. Mindful of this, the inspector knew he had to strike when and where he could, so wasted no time homing in on Franklin.

'Mr Franklin, you're fortunate enough to be able to afford the best representation in the country, to live in a mansion and to be feted and fawned over wherever you go. Because of that, and dare I say it, a certain lack of education, I fear you've lost your grip on reality. This isn't an episode out of Sherlock Holmes or Poirot where the police conduct their business over tea and scones in wealthy people's drawing rooms, this is a real life, or should I say, a real death, murder case, and so I'm gonna have to ask you to accompany me to the station.' Curzon turned to Baxter. 'How long did you say you'd been an *officer of the law* for again? Thirty-five years was it? All I can say is, you must have eaten a lot of infected beef during the early Nineties, coz this,' he pointed at a gobsmacked-looking Franklin, 'is a local football player, not a head of state, you pompous arsehole. In this country, as far as I'm aware, they get treated the same as everybody else, no matter what you and my superiors might think.'

A furious Baxter opened his mouth to protest but Curzon shot him down, calmly and with maximum irritation factor in his manner.

'I've got nothing to say to you, you coprophagous maggot.'

Then he let his phone ring out once to the detainment vehicle, which was the cue for Deegan and McKay to come in and assist him.

The detainment van was going to serve a purpose as Curzon's mobile interview room, because he knew that the moment he arrived at the police station, his superiors – already being phoned by Baxter – would command him to release Franklin. In truth, Curzon had accepted that he wasn't going to get anything out of the footballer, but he wanted to punish him and his lawyer for their arrogance, thinking they could just summon him to their manor, tell him how it was going to be and then dismiss him like a butler. If Franklin did do it, then he, Curzon, was determined to be his judge, because by the looks of things, nobody else was going to be.

Handcuffed, Franklin was put in the detention cage inside the vehicle, where he was all alone in the twilight for the first minute of the journey, until the van stopped at traffic lights and Curzon climbed out from the front and climbed into the back, locking himself up in the cage and sitting down opposite the celebrity. Thereon, McKay just drove and drove while his inspector subjected the footballer to some psychological needling.

'Mr Franklin, you've played in the top flight of professional football for over a decade. Now, that's no mean feat. You've had to shoulder barge your way through hundreds of other teenage boys in order to get to youth team level and then you've had to be single-minded and ruthless enough to claw your way into the big time. That must require an enormous amount of self-belief?'

Franklin responded by nodding, his large Adam's apple bobbing like a fishing weight, before he sighed deeply, betraying immense nervousness and fear.

'I mean,' Curzon continued, 'I'd imagine you'd have to consider yourself special even to embark upon such a journey. It goes without saying really that you'd need to consider yourself better than the rest of us, otherwise you'd be a fraud wouldn't you, somebody who's not what they seem, if you see what I'm getting at?' The footballer screwed his face up in confusion. 'So what are you Mr Franklin?'

'Sorry?'

'Are you a fraud or do you consider yourself better than the rest of us mortals who've donned football shirts at one time or another.'

'Better I suppose...obviously.'

'That's interesting, Mr Franklin, because you know, a lot of murderers think they're better than everyone else too. They think they have the right to take other folks lives, because other folk are less worthy than they are. They believe that they are above the rules and laws that govern the rest of us, moral and legal, because *they – are – special.* Is that you Mr Franklin?'

Franklin sighed again, so tremulously it sounded like he was shivering on a cold day.

'But it's not quite that simple, Mr Franklin. Interestingly enough, it's only when these people who think they're extraordinary commit murders that they learn they're actually frauds, that they've been deluding themselves all along, that they aren't special after all, because they, thank God, like ninety-nine point nine per cent of mankind, actually feel excruciating guilt for what they've done and want to repent. It's a very humbling thing is murder. In many ways I have more sympathy for the murderer than for his victim, because, let's face it, it's over for the victim. But for the murderer, it just goes on and on, this ever-increasing burden that they'd give anything to be lightened.' Curzon blew his cheeks out and shook his head as if daunted by just thinking about it. 'Yes, I've always tried to have compassion for murderers...except for the psychopaths of course, no point feeling sorry for them, they wouldn't recognise or appreciate it anyway...and they'd certainly never feel sorry for me!'

Curzon laughed out loud and looked at Franklin as if expecting reciprocal amusement. When he eventually stopped, he sighed contentedly and stared into the middle distance, spooking his prisoner in the process.

'Do you know what I've found, Mr Franklin? I've found it's the ones who own up without being caught, without having to be confronted with the evidence first that fare better in the long run. Of course, it always plays better with the judge, but, more importantly, yes, they may still be killers, but they at least have their dignity. It's the sneaking around, the degradation of lying to their fellow men that compounds the misery for those who wait to be proven guilty. That's almost as difficult to live with later on, once the initial survival adrenaline has worn off. Because, you see, to live the rest of your life without any pride, honour or integrity, is akin to living the rest of your life like a worm. What I'm trying to say is: murderers can still have honour.' And with that he banged on the side of the vehicle three times, causing it to draw to a halt. 'I'm going back up front, to give you time on your own to think about that. When I get back in this cage, I'm going to sit in silence for five minutes and give you the opportunity to start proceedings. If you haven't spoken after that then I'll have to be rude and blunt and confront you with what I know.'

Curzon stared into Franklin's eyes with a solid but convincingly compassionate look. For that brief moment, when all that each could see was the other's eyes, Curzon spoke very slowly and very deliberately.

'Think of the long term. Think of your honour. Think of your soul.'

He unlocked the cage and climbed out of the vehicle, repairing to the front seat, where he remained for another ten minutes before being dropped off outside a whitewashed retirement bungalow in the middle-class suburb of Newton Mearns, on the southern fringe of the city.

Chapter 15

Deegan and McKay stayed in the vehicle, while Curzon knocked three times at the door of the bungalow. With no one having answered, he walked round the side of the property to the back garden, where a white-haired, soft-faced lady of eighty was pruning her rose bushes.

'Hello Miss Anderson!'

The old lady turned from what she was doing.

'Ooh…you gave me a fright. It's enough to give an old woman a coronary.'

She spoke in one of those posh, middle-class Scottish accents, over-emphasising her R's.

'Sorry Miss Anderson, but I did knock.'

The old lady, wearing navy-blue polyester trousers and a pink summer top, came steadily across the lawn to meet him, removing her gardening gloves as she did so.

'Don't worry your wee head about it Patrick. I must be going deaf.' She smiled affectionately. 'Would you like a cup of tea?'

'That would be very nice Miss Anderson, thank you.'

Curzon spoke in a very soft, well-mannered and considerate tone, a tone reserved exclusively for this one old lady.

The old headmistress at his primary school, Miss Anderson was the only person in the policeman's life that he'd ever liked or trusted. When every other teacher had washed their hands of him, no doubt being repulsed by the mildew smell from his squalid clothes and the stale piss on his puny body, this childless spinster had taken him under her wing, even putting him up in her house when things got really bad at home. He always visited her before concluding a big case, because he needed to feel that sense of safety and security in her company to give him the courage to charge a man with murder. As a child he'd had no self-belief whatsoever. In fact, after years of mental abuse at the hands of a drunken father he was as nervous as a meerkat. But Miss Anderson had cured all that. She'd stroked his delicate curly head and caressed his slouching back in the cute school jumper she'd bought, filling him full of praise at the slightest achievement until he was, though never a sociable creature, at least a confident little misanthrope.

Curzon followed Miss Anderson into her large kitchen and sat down at the round, Formica-topped table, listening to her speak as she made tea.

'So, tell me Patrick, what have you been up to? Have you found yourself a nice girl to settle down with yet?'

'No Miss Anderson. The answer's still no just like every other month when you've asked me for the past twenty years.'

'Well, I happen to think it would do you good, that's all.'

She poured hot water from the kettle into two mugs, her own a plain white one, Curzon's an ancient, chipped specimen with Kojak on the side, a bubble next to his mouth filled with the words: *Who loves you baby?* This was a conduit he'd been drinking from round at her house ever since the age of eight, while the plate of Jammie Dodgers she brought to his table along with the tea were also a childhood favourite of the detective's.

'I do wish you'd find yourself a nice wife,' the old lady persisted.

'No Miss Anderson, the only woman in my life is you, you know that.'

Miss Anderson sat down and placed a liver-spotted hand on top of Curzon's. 'I'm not going to be around for ever my little chicken, and I'd hate to think I'd left you here all alone.'

'Don't talk like that Miss Anderson, please.'

Curzon looked and sounded genuinely distressed at this, so much that Miss Anderson felt compelled to stroke his curly hair back with her other hand to comfort him.

'Well, I'd like to know there was somebody good looking after you all the same. I think you'd like that too, only you're frightened of opening up for fear of being hurt.'

Curzon, who was now staring down at the table top, eager for some distraction from such a searching topic, rummaged around in the inside pocket of his suit jacket.

'I almost forgot,' he said, producing a pair of pruning secateurs he'd stolen from Alistair Meaks' shop. 'I saw these and thought of you and the rose bushes.'

'Oh Patrick, what are we going to do with you? I do hope you haven't taken these from somebody without asking?' She looked at him interrogatively, but with a glint of amusement in her eyes. 'Remember when you were a little boy? I was constantly apologising to parents for you taking other kids' stuff. You were like a cat bringing dead mice home.' She started laughing. 'And you've not changed a bit have you? Why do you do it? You're cutting your own nose off behaving like this Patrick, pre-empting people's enmity before they even have a chance to get to know you.'

'There's no one out there worth knowing Miss Anderson, you've got to believe me. If you'd seen a hundredth of the things I have to deal with, you wouldn't be such a positivist.'

'Even so, it's such a waste of a life, all this spitefulness you engage in. I should feel flattered that you've always been nice to me, I suppose.'

'Indeed. What's the point in having a nice person be nice to you, it's worthless, coz they're nice to everybody and it reflects on you in no way whatsoever. But when a nasty, spiteful person's nice to you, one way or another that's really got to mean something, right?'

Miss Anderson laughed and rubbed his hair again. 'Oh Patrick, what would we do without you, eh?'

Curzon stayed at Miss Anderson's for about half an hour, running the salient details of the murder case by her and hanging on the old woman's every word of advice, without which he never took any major decisions. Once they'd both agreed on what course of action he should take, she gave him a long, warm hug in which he always crumbled like a cookie and had to rush away from afterwards without looking back, for fear of having his tears detected.

Chapter 16

It took Curzon several minutes to wipe away all evidence of his emotions, before climbing back into the rear of the police vehicle, where he again sat opposite a by now weary and wary-looking Tommy Franklin. After banging on the side of the van, it pulled off and the detective sat silently in the twilight for five minutes without even making a conspicuous body movement, almost like a waxwork dummy. This made Franklin so uncomfortable that he dropped his head guiltily, unable to face the policeman. Suddenly, bang on the five-minute mark, Curzon jolted to as if woken from a trance and smiled congenially at his prisoner, like a bank manager about to grant a loan.

'So, you've decided to gamble your pride, your honour and your soul on the survival strategy have you? The keep lying and hope I get out of here approach.'

Franklin looked up for a moment but was unable to maintain eye contact with his interrogator, so bowed his head again.

'Do you know what I know about you?' Curzon continued. 'I know that you like the company of young boys.'

Franklin's head suddenly sprang up and he screwed his nose into an affected display of mock perplexity and shock.

'I also know that you made an unsuccessful sexual pass at Bobby McQueen when he was an apprentice at St. Clyde, and, in order to cover your tracks and avoid the embarrassment of having to face the lad again, you fabricated a story about him stealing from the players' dressing room, so that he got kicked out of the club.'

Curzon looked to one side, shaking his head as if it were genuinely causing him great pain to have to reveal these things, before looking back again to find a very different Franklin, pale now to the point of being white, tears welling up in his eyes.

'You were shocked to see Bobby turn up at Ms Fuchs' party. I mean, what reason would a young schemie have to be hanging round with the Hyndland set? Fair play to you, even though you've not donned a pair of boots for a while now, you were quick on your feet.

You darted away from that barbeque area at the speed of light, before the lad had chance to recognise and out you in front of your pals. You hid in the area beneath the front door steps, having one of your sneaky, gold-filtered Thai cigarettes, working out your next move. From here you saw Bobby McQueen come storming out, the unfortunate lad being under the misapprehension that he was pursuing young Monika, though she had in fact hidden in her mother's house. So, thinking it safe, you returned to the barbeque. With your sous-chef away consoling Matilda Fuchs in her study, you were all alone until – horror of horrors – Bobby reappeared to retrieve the wraps of cocaine he'd accidentally dropped there. Finally, it was just you and him, for the first time since you'd ruined his career at St. Clyde and ended all hope. You tried to hide yourself, busying around, bent double picking things off the floor behind the grill, but, bugger of all buggers, you're just too damned distinguishable and he spotted you.' Curzon's smile actually looked warm now, as if he were reminiscing about something pleasant. He stopped talking and stared gently into Franklin's eyes for about ten seconds before saying: 'Remember me?'

Franklin's eyes suddenly seemed to bulge out of his head in horror, while his right leg began to shake pneumatically.

'That's what he said wasn't it? *Remember me?*' Smiling, Curzon raised his eyebrows for a moment, trying to prompt a response from Franklin. 'Not content with having ruined the young lad's career, within a moment you would take his life.' Curzon's smile suddenly disappeared and, staring hard and aggressively into Franklin's steely blue pupils, searching for the man's soul, he looked like he could quite easily have been a killer himself. 'Not only were you petrified of this drunk and drugged-up young man exposing you to everyone at the party, but your ego was piquing you, wasn't it? You were angry because he'd spurned your advances that day at the football ground…you were furious with him at his cockiness, just swaggering round in front of you like that? Who was he to reject and, worse, have the drop on the great Tommy Franklin? Such was your rage, that, before you knew it, you'd picked up a breadknife, charged out of the barbeque area and plunged it into the young man's chest. Was he dead or still alive? We'll never know, because you wrapped him up in the blue tarpaulin onto which he'd fallen and left him there until the party ended, when you carried him out over your big, weightlifter's shoulders – still mummified in plastic – and put him into the back of your Range Rover along with your barbeque equipment and four heavy concrete bricks. Then, so as not to arouse attention, you drove at neutral speed down to Largs, put the body on your boat at the Yacht Haven there, attached a backpack, placed the four bricks inside, before sailing out to sea and tossing the poor fellow overboard. But it turned out that you're not the best after all, because mother nature kicked your effort into touch by spewing Bobby back onto the beach.' At this point Curzon's mouth formed into a furious rictus and he spoke through clenched teeth, causing him to sound like a really poor ventriloquist. 'Feel. Free. To. Take. The. Floor. Whenever. You. See. Fit.'

'I've nothing to say.'

Encouraged by this response from his prisoner, Curzon deployed a white lie.

'I suppose you want to know where we've just been, while you were sat back here in the dark on your own?' Franklin, who was no doubt disorientated, nodded, probably involuntarily. 'We've just been on your boat, talking to forensics…and guess what?'

'What?' Franklin replied in an eager manner.

'They've already found lots of particles from the concrete bricks all over the deck.'

'That dust must have got on my shoes while I was doing the barbeque…it means nothing.'

'It means that you've been on the boat between last Saturday night and today,' Curzon said, smugly, so smugly in fact that handcuffed Franklin, immediately realising his mistake, lunged across the metre of distance between them and headbutted the detective, right on the nose. With the full weight of this iron-pumping athlete now lying on top of him, Curzon just about managed to bang out his distress code on the side of the cage, causing the vehicle to screech to a halt before both Deegan and McKay burst in through the back doors. Problem was, Curzon had the key to the cage in his back pocket, so they were actually powerless to prevent him from being suffocated and merely had to resort to talking Franklin off, which thankfully worked.

Blood gushing from his nose, Curzon stumbled out of the cage, then, with trembling hands he locked the door behind him.

'You've blown your one and only chance Franklin! Now you're a murderer and a man without honour too – you're a worm!'

The vehicle was now parked on a busy street, so to say that Curzon was making a spectacle would be an understatement as old ladies doing their shopping stopped to gawp inside. Deegan and McKay shepherded him out, but before they'd managed to close the doors he was still shouting in the street, Franklin staring out of his cage like some Victorian freak show.

'This is just the beginning Franklin! When the adrenaline of survival wears off, you've got an eternity of self-loathing and guilt to confront, coz you're a fraud Franklin! You're not one of the best at all, you're a phoney and in time you'll be found out by yourself…and that's the scariest revelation of all!'

If nothing else, at least Curzon had a legitimate excuse for taking Franklin in now. However, when he got back to the police station, Fergus Baxter was already there, along with an apoplectic chief superintendent, wanting to know how the prisoner had arrived over an hour after his lawyer, even though they'd left for the station at the same time. Backed up by DS Deegan and DC McKay, Curzon claimed to have been held hostage by his suspect in the back of the detainment vehicle, while his colleagues had had to pull over to negotiate his release. Of course, the superintendent immediately asked why they'd not brought the vehicle straight to the station where, not only would they have had more people to deal with the situation, but also a spare key for the cage. Curzon admitted that, in hindsight, the latter approach now seemed the obvious course of action but, alas, such lack of foresight and lateral thinking probably explained why he wasn't chief superintendent and his interlocutor was. Now, you might be wondering how it's possible that a superintendent would tolerate such blatant impudence and insubordination. Well, when you just happen to have a son who's been filmed snorting and dealing cocaine, while openly bragging about the fact that his father – then a chief inspector – supplies him with drugs confiscated on raids, it's not that hard to fathom, especially if copies of the footage are stored in several lawyers' safety deposit boxes, to be opened in the event of Curzon suffering an unnatural death or dismissal from the force.

As a PC, Curzon had spent all his spare time investigating and keeping everyone around him and above him under surveillance, hiding bugs in police vehicles, police-frequented pubs and golf clubs, while filming officers and their families performing embarrassing or criminal activities. You see, that's why he had the edge, because he wasn't in the job for the money, he just wanted to be a copper twenty-four hours a day, every day, and he accumulated pointless tittle-tattle on people in the same way he collected the worthless, personal bric-a-brac hoarded in his apartment. He'd never gone on the offensive with his stockpile of ammunition though, using it only as a deterrent. For example, he was only blackmailing Chief Superintendent Barney Clark now, after Clark – then an inspector – had tried to scapegoat Curzon over a batch of ecstasy that had gone missing during a dawn raid, when the latter was just starting out as a sergeant. Far from ruining Curzon's career though, the corrupt policeman had merely provided our *hero* with the justification he'd needed to capitalise on the info he had stored, which resulted in him filling the chief inspector's post the moment Clark moved up to superintendent. However, in this instance, even though Curzon was adamant that Franklin was their man, orders from above compelled Clark to command his inspector to release the football star and charge Craig Hunter, who had a plethora of evidence stacked against him and had always been their obvious prime suspect.

'As a force, our priority is to get somebody into the dock following a murder, so as to reassure the public that we're protecting them. That's not going to happen if you pursue Franklin, coz there's no concrete evidence and his representatives will make our lives hell. Your job isn't to judge, it's merely to offer the procurator fiscal whatever evidence you find. Now, there's plenty of that against Hunter, so let them take responsibility for the rest. If you don't do it then I'll have to find someone who will.'

As Curzon was opening the door to leave Clark's office, the superintendent mitigated his tone and tried to protect himself from any repercussions:

'Of course, I owe you one for this.'

Even though Curzon had given neutral testimony in court, at times doing the defence's job for them, the brick dust from the Castlemilk construction site and the CCTV footage from The Goose pub proved enough to see Craig Hunter sent down and hated in his community, his poor family receiving death threats and regularly having bricks hurled through their windows. And all because of Fergus Baxter and his cronies in high places who'd conspired, once again, to allow a rich murderer – first a banker and now a footballer – to walk free, while an innocent schemie went to prison as a smokescreen. 'What about the photograph albums!' I hear you scream. Well, Curzon had withheld these items, firstly because he'd gained them by dubious means, and secondly, they in themselves proved very little as regards this particular case, apart from illustrating his hunch. Mindful from the beginning that Franklin would probably get off, he'd reserved them as his own contingency form of justice. And so, on a freezing December night, just hours after Craig Hunter had been given a twenty-year jail sentence, Jackie the Junkie ran from bus stop to bus stop, in and out of pub toilets and down onto underground platforms, pasting copies of the former football star's holiday snaps on walls. Over the coming days, arguments would rage at bars and in work canteens between fans of one Glasgow team who couldn't accept the truth, and those of the other who would go on to compose abusive songs and chants that will no doubt remain in folklore for at least a generation. Indeed, such was the ignominy created by these images that Tommy Franklin had to leave his post as manager of St. Clyde F.C, sell his house and move to Thailand, leaving Curzon to worry that he'd probably done more harm than good with his little smear campaign.

While Jackie had been running from one side of the city to the other in the early hours, fly-posting in her jogging bottoms, face covered by her hooded jacket, the policeman had been doing what he did every time a case closed, whether victorious or not: he'd lost hundreds of pounds on a roulette wheel and drank a seemingly never-ending procession of whiskies. Once all his money had been squandered, he repaired to Nancy's plush townhouse at Park Circus, where he went to forget whatever hideous events he'd been absorbed in.

Curzon stood at Nancy's little bar with a bourbon on the rocks, donning his beige Burberry raincoat and a trilby hat, which she kept for him in the house. Meanwhile, the martini cocktail-sipping, seventy-year-old prostitute did nothing more than sit at a tall stool, side on to the counter, smelling of expensive perfume and looking aloof. With one leg crossed over the other, she was wearing a long, black, figure-hugging silk dress, a slit up one side revealing stockings and suspenders. As Miles Davis's lonely trumpet played on a CD in the background, she held a smoking cigarette away from her face in a holder, her slender hands gloved in black silk all the way up to her elbows and just beyond. Occasionally she'd fix a seductive stare on the detective, her hawk-like visage heavily lined and sagging, her strict, vein-marbled eyes, frighteningly pronounced in their coronas of black mascara. This whole grotesque effect was capped by an elbow-length, wavy brown wig and vivid red lipstick, a sight which would inspire terror in anyone except a drunk in a dimly-lit room. But she was the only woman Curzon had ever met who truly understood noir. Together, they would while away the small hours, acting out scenes from movies like *The Big Sleep* or *Pick Up On South Street*, which, as a young girl, she'd actually sneaked into the pictures to watch on the day of its release in 1953. Not only that, but he'd seen old sepia photographs of her as a twenty-year-old, when she'd first started out as an escort. Without a word of exaggeration they could quite easily have been stills from an Ava Gardner movie. If only he'd been born thirty years earlier, the DCI often thought, then even he: cold, repressed, insular Curzon, might have fallen head over heels in love with her. But fate deigned that he had arrived on this earth three decades too late for his soulmate, who had also escaped a miserable childhood through the imaginary world that we now call *noir*, a world that she'd strived to make real, for fear of having nowhere else to hide.

At four o'clock, after three hours of purely platonic role play, without one so much as touching the other, the prostitute and the detective, or should I say, the pro skirt and the peeper, enacted their usual farewell. Curzon clinked his whisky tumbler against her martini glass and said, with a slight hiccup:

'Here's lookin' at you kid!'

Then he drained the remainder of his drink, removed his trilby hat, placed it on the bar and left the building unsteadily. He stumbled down the frosty steps from the townhouse, before staggering across the sparkling street to a moonlit park, where he slumped on a bench and smoked a cigarette, while tilting his head back to enjoy the stars.

GUILT TRIPPER

(Kindle Edition)

Set in Scotland, Guilt Tripper is the fast-moving story of Glasgow man, Danny White, an unemployed artist whose beautiful girlfriend has left him for his successful and wealthy best friend, Bob Fitzgerald. Convinced his socialist beliefs have made him soft, Danny decides things should change. So when he discovers Fitzgerald has a perverted violent side, he extorts money from him which he then uses to set up an art school in the Scottish Highlands for underprivileged teenagers.

Everything is perfect until a bedraggled Fitzgerald turns up at the school one night and tells Danny the sinister truth about the money funding his project. Horrified and conscience-stricken, Danny attempts to put things right - but is it all too late?

Direct Amazon links:

www.amazon.com/dp/B0091BAM8Y **(US and Worldwide)**

Published by The Electronic Book Company
www.theelectronicbookcompany.com
Language: UK English Spellings

Back to the contents page